WILD HEARTS OF SUMMER

WILD HEARTS OF SUMMER

OCEAN CITY BOARDWALK SERIES
BOOK 3

DONNA FASANO

Wild Hearts of summer

Paperback ISBN: 978-1-939000-40-8

eBook ISBN: 978-1-939000-41-5

Find the author:

Facebook – Facebook.com/DonnaFasanoAuthor

Twitter – Twitter.com/DonnaFaz

Pinterest – Pinterest.com/DonnaFaz

Instagram – Instagram.com/Donna_Fasano

Contents

Cathy Whitley's two best friends, Sara and Heather, may have found the men of their dreams... and that's all well and good for them. But that's not going to happen to Cathy. She allowed love to catch her off-guard once and it drained her, body and soul. She'll never let it happen again. Ever.

Brad Henderson has been chasing Cathy for years. He's settled for their on-again-off-again, "friends with bennies" relationship for far longer than he expected. Attempting to navigate the rip currents surrounding her heart has left him swimming in circles.

Then Brad inherits a business from billionaire Harold Hopewell. Hopewell had traveled the world and was touched by the stories of the people he met. In death, Hopewell is giving back, leaving an unusual will filled *with life-altering bequests. Brad is stunned and wonders if his new life will draw Cathy closer—or push her further out of reach.*

One way or the other, it's time to draw a line in the sand...

THE INHERITANCE LETTER

———

Layton, Felder, Bach & Moore
Attorneys-at-Law
58 East 42nd Street, Suite 1800
New York, New York 10016

Bradley D. Henderson
13 Cormorant Street
Ocean City, MD 21842

Dear Mr. Henderson,

I am acting as the executor of the estate of Mr.

———

Harold Hopewell, whose Last Will and Testament was entered into probate in the Surrogate's Court, New York County, State of New York. I write to inform you of certain assets bequeathed to you pursuant to Mr. Hopewell's Last Will and Testament, to wit:

The miniature golf and arcade center located at 1 Stargrass Avenue, Ocean City, MD, all contents located on the property, as well as the land the business sits on.

I have enclosed a deed to the property, the business license which has been transferred into your name, and an inventory of items in the buildings and on the grounds.

You may be wondering why Mr. Hopewell would name you in his will. I will do my best to explain. Nearly twenty years ago, Mr. Hopewell happened to see your interview in the documentary entitled *Ocean City Beach Patrol: Then and Now*. Even though you were just a teen at the time, Mr. Hopewell was impressed with your earnest enthusiasm for beach safety and ocean rescue. About ten years later, Mr. Hopewell and two youngsters were involved in a boating accident and were saved from drowning by a member of a water rescue team. The incident reminded him of you, and he visited Ocean City for a Beach Patrol tour, requesting you as his guide. He was greatly affected by the fact that your dedication to saving lives has never faltered over the years and he wanted you to know he not only noticed but highly respected your chosen profession.

Please do not hesitate to contact me with any questions.

Regards,

Frederick Bach, Esquire

PROLOGUE

Blazing summer sunlight beat down on Brad Henderson's head as he loped along the sweltering asphalt pavement. Sweat saturated his t-shirt and his legs felt lead-heavy. Less than a quarter mile to go. All he could think about was the cool shower and the icy pitcher of water waiting for him at home. He glanced over at his running buddy, Jack Barclay.

Seven years Brad's junior, Jack ran with his shoulders back, his chin up, and... hell, the guy was actually smiling. Brad would have laughed if he wasn't so focused on dragging air into his lungs.

The early August sky was a clear, azure dome, the sun a white-hot disk overhead. The intense heat rolling up from the roadway made breathing difficult. He and Jack ran after sunset when they could, but Jack had a beach wedding to set up later and Brad had a meeting to finalize the plans for the Beach Patrol fundraiser that would benefit a local boy who was battling a rare form of brain cancer.

They turned onto Cormorant Street and both of them broke stride. Brad gasped and wiped his brow with his forearm as he walked toward his bungalow at the end of the street. Sweat dripped from his hair, running in rivulets down his neck.

"It's hot as an oven today," Jack said.

"And I'm a fully roasted turkey." The run had winded Brad to the point that he could barely get the words out. "Stick a fork in me already."

Jack laughed. "Hey, you're not gettin' old on me, are you, pal? You know, thirty-five is almost middle aged."

"I kept up with you, didn't I?" Being razzed about his age was nothing new for Brad. With the majority of his team being under twenty, he was used to it.

"You did." His friend nodded. "You matched me stride for stride." Then Jack gave Brad a backhanded tap on his upper arm and asked, "Can we get inside? I need to whiz like a race horse."

In one smooth motion, Brad pulled the lanyard holding his house key from around his neck and tossed it to Jack. "Let yourself in the back door. I'm going to grab the mail." His friend jogged across the yard, and Brad called, "There's filtered water in the fridge. Beer, too, if you'd rather have that."

Jack lifted his hand in thanks and disappeared around the corner of the house.

Brad paused at the mailbox which, thankfully, was shaded by a leafy crepe myrtle that should have been cut back last fall, but he'd never gotten around to it. Several bees buzzed among the profusion of brilliant crimson blooms. He rested his hands on his hips and gave himself a minute to catch his breath. The expanse of bay behind the house looked smooth-as-glass. Several sailboats, a couple of pontoons, and a dozen or so jet skis were too far away for their engines to be anything more than low, wobbling rumbles. And he counted six parachutes floating on air behind tow boats.

No doubt about it, the summer tourist season was in full swing.

Ocean City, Maryland offered plenty of fun in the sun. People from all over the northeastern United States felt it was the *only* vacation destination for beach-loving folks.

It was days like this one—clear-skied, full-on sunny, fiery-hot scorchers—that chased the boaters out onto the water and had the sun-worshipers crowding the sandy beaches. Brad had been born and raised in this tourist town; he'd grown up in the same little house on the bay he now lived in. Ocean City had provided him and his parents with a good life. Hardly a summer day passed that he wasn't swimming in the sea, surfing the waves, paddle boarding on the bay, or sitting in a lifeguard stand, keeping watch over vacationers. He felt fortunate that he'd turned his love of the water into an occupation he could devote himself to, body and soul.

The piercing cry of a gull nudged him out of his reverie. He tugged open the mailbox, scooped up the pile of envelopes that had been neatly wrapped in a grocery store flyer, and then jogged toward the back deck. His thoughts on a glass of cold water to quench his thirst, he caught the toe of his running shoe on the topmost wooden step, and a couple of the envelopes slid from the pile. He balanced himself and caught the letters before they tumbled to the ground.

The official-looking return address on one of the envelopes captured his attention and halted his forward progress.

Layton, Felder, Bach & Moore. Attorneys-At-Law. New York, New York.

His brow furrowed as he stuck his pinkie under the envelope's glued flap and ripped it open. He pulled out the bundle of papers, and after scanning to the second paragraph of the cover letter, he stopped reading. His stomach fluttered strangely, and his knees went so weak he moved to the patio chair and sat down.

Adrenalin shot through his body; his ears rang and his heart thudded in his chest. He glanced across the bay. Surely, he'd misread the words. Or opened someone else's mail. He flipped over the manila envelope.

There it was. As plain as those pesky phragmites growing along the shoreline of his backyard.

Bradley D. Henderson.

The sound of the heavy glass door sliding open caused Brad to look up just as Jack stepped out onto the deck.

"Hey, I brought you some water." Jack took several steps toward Brad, holding out his offering. "Dude, what's wrong?" He set both glasses on a nearby table. "You look like somebody died."

Brad blinked and glanced back down at the letter. "Yeah. Apparently, somebody did." He paused to swallow, but nerves had turned his mouth to cotton. "I didn't know him. I don't think I did, anyway. But he left me a flippin' fortune."

He lifted the letter so Jack could read for himself. Brad could barely believe what he'd read.

Who was this Harold Hopewell? And why would he leave Brad an arcade?

"Whoa!" Jack exclaimed, his excitement barely contained. "Would you look at that? You're rich! The arcade on Stargrass Avenue! *Dude!* The land alone must be worth a million dollars."

Brad felt like he was in a thick fog. He nodded.

"That place has been closed for the past six months, right? Maybe longer."

"Yeah," Jack said. "There was talk about it at a City Council meeting back in the spring. I remember residents were asking what was going on, and the Council promised to look into it. No one's said a word since that I know of."

The deed to the property that Brad held in his hand was covered in fancy brown cardstock, latched together at the top with a heavy metal fastener.

"So who *was* this guy?" Jack asked. "And why would he name you in his will?" Before Brad could answer, Jack continued, "It says here he saw you on some documentary. What's that all about?"

"It was years ago. The first summer I was hired," Brad told him, squinting against the sunlight that seemed to suddenly grow brighter. "I was interviewed for a documentary about the history of the OC Beach Patrol. As the newest member of the team, they wanted to talk to me."

"What were you... eighteen?"

"Seventeen," Brad corrected. "I'd just earned my certification, and I was cocky as hell."

The Ocean City Beach Patrol manned the

lifeguard stands along the town's ten mile stretch of beach. Brad hadn't missed a single summer working as a guard in all these years.

"I took a lot of crap for that interview," he murmured.

Jack didn't respond, but curiosity tilted his head.

"The interviewer asked me what I wanted to do when I grew up," Brad explained. "I was a kid. What the hell did I know at the time? I blurted out the first thing that came to mind. That I'd love to own a mini golf business." Despite the irritating memory, he couldn't help but bark out a single, low laugh. "Everybody on the patrol team called me Putt-Putt for months. I didn't think I'd ever live that down."

Both men were quiet for a few seconds while Jack took the opportunity to take a swig of water. "Ah, so it's not the arcade that's the important bit. It's the golf course. This Harold Hopewell was making your dream come true, maybe?"

The observation made as much sense as any, Brad decided. He tugged his phone out of the band strapped around his upper arm and he connected to the internet with a few short swipes. A quick web search of Howard Hopewell caused him to let out a long, low whistle.

"Apparently, this guy was a billionaire," he told Jack. "A venture capitalist, it says here, whatever the hell that is. Married. Wife died young. No kids. He never remarried. Hell, looks like the guy had more money than Bill Gates."

Jack looked up from reading the letter. "According to this lawyer, you met Hopewell. You spent the day with him, in fact."

"I did?" Brad looked up from the screen on his phone. "That has me stumped. Wait a minute, though." He nodded. "Yeah. I vaguely remember spending the day with an old guy. But it was years ago. *Years*. At least ten. Maybe more. From what I remember, he was nice enough. Wanted to know all about my job. The saves I'd made." Brad shook his head. "But he was just a normal person, you know? Not eccentric or anything. Nothing about him said billionaire, that's for sure." Brad looked off toward the bay. "I guess that was Hopewell? Had to be, right?"

Jack was busy guzzling more water.

"Listen, Jack," Brad said, "don't say anything about this to anyone, okay?"

"You got it," Jack assured him. "Your secret's safe with me."

Setting his iPhone aside, Brad picked up the deed again and marveled at how his life was about to change.

"I wonder what Cathy will say," he murmured automatically.

"What? You think Cathy Whitley is going to be impressed?" Jack guffawed. "Didn't the two of you argue just last week because she said you shouldn't be living in your parents' house?"

That hadn't been an argument, Brad thought. That had merely been a lively conversation. Or it had started out that way, at least. Cathy had a way of getting under his skin. In more ways than one. And he did the same to her. They were like oil and water far too often. But sometimes, they were like a perfectly seasoned salad dressing—an ideal blend of spicy and sweet in a flawless amalgamation. The thought made his mouth twist wryly.

Being a chef, she would thoroughly appreciate the analogy, he realized.

"She might have a point," Jack said. "About you living here—"

"It's not like they live here, Jack. Mom and Dad

retired to Boca Raton two years ago," Brad said. "And I pay them rent."

"Hey, man—" Jack lifted his hands, palms out "—I don't need an explanation. I'm just saying... Cathy is..." He shrugged. "Cathy." Then he winced. "Sorry, bro. Really. I know you've been chasing that woman for years. I'm just not so sure she'll ever be up for getting caught."

Jack was right. Cathy was Cathy. Honest-to-a-fault, hard-working, responsible, no-filter, say-it-like-it-is-even-if-it-hurts. And skittish as hell when it came to their relationship.

She was one of a kind. Thank God.

And that redhead drove him nuts.

When things between them were good, they were *very* good. But when they weren't, life could be a nightmare.

Brad smoothed his thumb back and forth across the deed of the business he now owned. This unmitigated good fortune would certainly change his life. Maybe it would change Cathy's life, too.

If he played his cards right, maybe...

His mind churned with possibilities.

Just... maybe.

CHAPTER ONE

Tears rolled down Cathy Whitley's cheeks and she sniffed, even though she knew doing so would only make matters worse for her.

"What's wrong over there, missy?"

The sarcastic question came from Lyle, one of Cathy's long-time customers. The bewhiskered old cuss sat at the counter, his short, pudgy fingers laced around a heavy ceramic coffee mug. All he needed was an eye patch to be a dead ringer for a pirate.

"You look like you lost your best friend."

Al, the "Frick" to Lyle's "Frack," voiced this observation. With his black-rimmed glasses, neatly trimmed beard, and normally polite manner, Al brought to mind a scholar on holiday—or a nutty professor, depending on his mood.

The men came in for breakfast each morning, and most days, they stayed through lunch. They found all manner of subjects to discuss, from politics and religion, to world events, real estate, music, movies, even the Hollywood insiders, but usually this was a topic of a last resort. Their debate sessions were, for the most part, entertaining; they were also multifarious, as she'd learned from her favorite learning tool, Dictionary.com's Word of the Day. However, let the slightest lull slow their conversation and both men delighted in teasing Cathy, her wait staff, even other customers; anyone who seemed the slightest bit susceptible became their prey.

They meant no harm, Cathy knew that. They were just two oldsters whiling away their retirement years in the most entertaining way they could find. She didn't let them bother her. Showing the least bit of insult or annoyance would only encourage a ramping up of the pestering commentary.

Al's mention of losing a friend made her thoughts turn to Heather. Cathy couldn't believe it had been nearly three months since her friend had talked to her. The longing that blew through Cathy was quickly shadowed by the hurt that pinched her heart. She chased the thought out of her mind as if it were a gaggle of noisy geese, too busy to dwell on it right now.

Cathy tossed Lyle and Al a bright smile, and then she focused her gaze back to her cutting board, making short work of mincing the onion before scooping up the pile and dropping it into the glass bowl. She stepped over to the sink, washed and dried her hands, and grabbed a paper napkin to blot her cheeks.

Before moving on to the next chore, she took a moment to glance out at the dining room. Every table was occupied, and the room was abuzz with the sounds of people enjoying breakfast; cutlery scraping against ceramic tableware, laughter, and the hum of a dozen different private conversations filling the air.

The Sunshine Café was her pride and joy. She'd

had to hire six extra people to wait tables this summer because of the wonderful swarm of tourists, and she'd hired two part-time short order cooks so she wouldn't feel so overwhelmed. It was nice to know she could take a day off through the week if she wanted. Business was better than good, and she was damned relieved about that. Owning a restaurant, or *any* business in a tourist town for that matter, could be iffy from each season to the next. Cathy was grateful that this summer Ocean City was teeming with tourists; seaside visitors packed the place for breakfast and lunch, the two meals she served each day, and even the local residents continued to show up on a regular basis.

The front door opened, and she smiled a cheerful hello when Sara walked in.

"Morning," Sara sang, waving to the staff and to Al and Lyle, as she waddled toward the counter, balancing a platter full of warm cinnamon buns.

Over eight months pregnant, Sara Carson ran the sweet shop next to Cathy's café. The women had been friends for many years. In fact, they attended grade school together. Along with Heather Phillips, the owner of the Lonely Loon B&B upstairs, the women had been called everything from the three little piglets to a three ring circus. Cathy's favorite times had been when they'd gone out together to get three sheets to the wind. But Heather's anger at Cathy continued to hold fast, even after all these weeks. Again, Cathy shoved the miserable thought from her mind because she knew, unfortunately, she was fully responsible for every ounce of ire Heather leveled on her.

The rich, buttery aroma of the buns made Cathy's mouth water. "Gosh, they smell good, Sara, and they look scrumptious." She moved to the counter, lifted the top off the large, domed glass serving dish, and began stacking the buns on the pedestal plate.

"Sorry I'm late," Sara said. "I didn't sleep well last night. Contractions woke me up several times."

Startled, Cathy went still. "Contractions? But it's too soon, isn't it?"

Sara shook her head. "We're all good. It's normal. Doctor Jacobs called them Braxton Hicks contractions. My body's just getting ready for the main event."

Relieved at the news, Cathy grinned when she

thought about the soon-to-arrive bundle of joy. She couldn't wait to be an auntie.

"I'll take one of those buns," Al called.

"Me, too," Lyle said. "Put it on Al's bill. He owes me one."

Cathy continued to fill the pedestal plate. "Just hold your horses, gentlemen. I'll be right there."

"Listen," Sara said, "I need to run. I've got to get Heather's order up to her. Her guests are going to want breakfast."

The mention of Heather caused Cathy's mouth to purse and she cut her gaze toward the floor, staring at the toes of her shoes as she tried to swallow away her reaction. Emotion burned her eye sockets just as sharply as the onions had done just moments before. What the hell was wrong with her? She'd become fairly practiced at tamping down the misery she felt over the situation. Why was this causing her such grief today?

Heaving a sigh, she looked at Sara.

"Oh, honey," Sara whispered, touching Cathy's shoulder, "I'm sorry."

"Does she *ever* mention me?"

Sara's silent, pained expression said it all.

"Cathy, why won't you let me talk to her?" Sara asked.

"Absolutely not." Cathy left two buns on Sara's platter and replaced the dome on the glass pedestal dish. "She has to get over this on her own. I don't want you to push her."

"Okay. I won't." Sara reached around and rubbed at the small of her back. "I don't know that it'll help how you're feeling, but she really *has* been overwhelmed. In a good way, of course. The Loon is full, and Daniel's been busy writing, so Heather's taking care of Mia."

Over the winter, Daniel Atwell had stayed at The Loon, and he and Heather had become a couple. Daniel and his gorgeous, dark-eyed, five-year-old daughter Mia had moved to Ocean City back in the spring.

With a new man in her life, a new little family to get to know, Heather must be absolutely elated. Sadness tinged the smile that curled the corners of Cathy's mouth. She felt completely delighted for Heather; she only longed for the opportunity to be involved in her friend's newfound happiness.

"You know," Cathy murmured, "I don't want *you* pushing her, but there's no reason why I can't push her... right?" She reached into her back pocket for her phone before she lost her nerve.

Sara blinked. "What are you going to do?"

"What else? I'm pulling on my smartass pants. Heather's seen me wear them plenty of times before."

Orneriness skittered through her and she almost chuckled as she began the text message.

Cathy: We never know what tomorrow will bring.

Cathy: A tsunami. A massive earthquake.

Cathy: An invasion of zombies.

Cathy: You should forgive me before the world ends.

When Cathy's gaze met Sara's, her friend was grinning.

"Classic Cathy." Sara fairly sang the words.

"Damn right. If I can't wait her out, I'll wear her ass down."

Sara chuckled. "Go, you. Now, I really should run."

"Now *that*, missy, would be a sight to behold."

Sara's lips curled cheerfully. "Classic Cathy

really *is* making a comeback. Great! I've missed her."

So had Cathy. Playing the passive one had never been her style and she had no idea why she'd let this go on for so long. Having reached out to Heather, her mood lightened considerably.

Nodding toward the platter with the two buns on it, Cathy said, "I'll wash this up for you, Sara, and bring it over later."

"Thanks." Sara turned on her heel, waggling her fingers in the air. "Chat later."

"Have a good one!" Cathy called after her. The urge to whistle a perky tune curled in her belly as she transferred the cinnamon buns to small dessert plates. It felt satisfying to finally do something proactive about her situation with Heather. Cathy slid the buns in front of Al and Lyle. "Here you go, gentlemen. Enjoy these on the house," she told them. Then she grabbed the coffee pot to refresh their cups. The men gawked at her in silence.

Narrowing her gaze at them, she asked, "Do you want the buns or not?"

Her tone snapped them out of their stupor.

"What's the matter with you, Lyle?" Al

blustered as he snatched up his napkin. "Eat your bun."

"Thanks, Cathy." Lyle picked up his fork and tucked in.

A server brought her an order ticket and slid it across the counter. "Two orders of eggs Benedict, one dressed, one naked. One short stack of blueberry pancakes with a side of bacon. And a BLT, extra crispy."

"Got it." Cathy picked up the slip of paper. Why anyone would want to eat eggs Benedict without the hollandaise sauce was beyond her, but she'd give the customer what they ordered.

"Hey!"

Cathy glanced up as Brad breezed through the door like visiting royalty, bringing with him a gust of salt-tinged summer air.

"People of the Sunshine Café! Good morning to you!"

Al, Lyle, and a couple other locals shouted out a greeting. Brad's arrival even had the tourists smiling.

Dressed in red swim trunks and a t-shirt—the official uniform of the OC Beach Patrol—Brad stood six-foot tall without an ounce of fat on his sleek swimmer's physique. Blond, blue-eyed, sun-bronzed, and as gorgeous as a tropical sunset, he was the epitome of the seaside lifeguard. The kind of man every woman dreamed would save her if she ever got in over her head.

The server who'd just turned in the breakfast order exhaled audibly, her cute, unguarded expression going all soft with possibility.

"Sheri," Cathy said, giving the seventeen-year-old's forearm a light tap with her index finger, "do you have customers waiting for coffee? Juice? Water?"

"Oh, yeah." Sheri's eyes went round. "Sorry, Cathy," she murmured as she hurried off toward the drink station.

Cathy moved to the kitchen, poured pancake batter on the hot griddle, popped bread into the toaster, and put eggs into a saucepan to poach.

Brad had that effect on females everywhere he went.

Many years ago when she'd attended high school, she'd dated him off and on. Cathy had hated how some girls had acted around him—gushing like geysers, chattering like chimps, simpering like simpletons. Bradley Henderson had her female school mates twisting themselves inside out and had laid waste to more BFFs than Cathy could count.

The assessment wasn't entirely fair to Brad, Cathy knew. What normal teen-aged male wouldn't play the field when he had a meadow-full of wildflowers waiting and eager to be plucked?

What she hated most was the memory of having acted like an idiot over him herself every time he'd found a new "steady" to wear his class ring. Oh, she hadn't gushed or chattered or simpered. That had never been her way. But she'd suffered her share of jealousy and teen angst back then, that was as certain as it was regrettable.

Since those innocent days though, she'd learned the hard lesson—no man was worth that kind of anxiety.

After she flipped the pancakes, she grabbed four warm plates, and set them on her work area. Then she fished the eggs from the poaching liquid.

Life had led Cathy to places outside Ocean City during her twenties, and while no one would ever call her six-year foray into marriage fortunate or lucky, she had returned to her home town five years ago a different person. More mature, more focused, determined to be self-sufficient. She couldn't thank Todd, her ex, for much, but he had forced her to realize she didn't need a man to feel whole. She could take care of herself. It had taken some time, but at the ripe old age of thirty-five, Cathy understood she was fine on her own.

Having broken free of that dark stage of her life, she'd run back to her family and friends seeking the fresh air of freedom, the care-free life of sun and sand, and gorgeous, easy-going Brad had seemed just the man to offer her that.

Their friendship had easily been rekindled. In fact, some would accuse them of being more than friends; and depending on the definition, that could very well be true. She and Brad did spend time together. She liked him. He made her laugh. And he sure as hell was easy on the eyes. If she ever found herself plagued by the blues, she would call him and he'd take her for a night on the town. The two of them even went so far as to scratch those very intimate itches that cropped up every now and again.

But when it came to Brad, or any man for that matter, Cathy kept her softer emotions in check. Under lock and key, really. She suffered not a wit of jealousy when women turned to stare at his tight butt or went all hazy-eyed when he shot them one of his million dollar smiles. She endured not even a smidge of envy when she saw him out and about with some attractive tourist he met on a Saturday night.

The toast popped and she plucked the golden brown bread from the slots, slathered two slices with a little mayo, and set them on one plate. She piled on extra crispy bacon, lettuce, and tomato, and cut the sandwich in half. Then she buttered the rest of the toast.

Cathy's eyes were wide open. Brad might be kind, considerate, warm-hearted, open-minded, intelligent, and fun-loving, but he was also a flirt, a Romeo, an alley cat constantly on the prowl. In other words, he was good friend material. Period.

Thank heavens she was looking for nothing more than that.

Scooping up the pancakes from the griddle, she arranged them on a plate and finished the eggs Benedict. Then she brought the food to the counter.

"Sheri, order's up!" she called.

Brad surprised her by rounding the corner of

the counter and coming toward her. Usually, he made a bee-line for the drink station where it was his habit to fill his insulated thermos with fresh coffee before heading out to a guard stand or the ATV, depending on his particular assignment for the day.

She couldn't help but smile when he grinned at her, his dimples were enough to make a weaker woman keel over.

"Morning, gorgeous," he murmured, setting down his thermos on the countertop.

Before she could speak, he slid his arms around her and kissed her like no one was watching.

CHAPTER TWO

His lips were warm, soft, familiar. And for several long seconds, the sensuous sensations swept Cathy away. The whooshing of blood through her ears, the sudden thudding of her pulse, drowned out the normal sounds of the café. The kiss ended as suddenly as it had begun, and she found herself being picked up off her feet. Brad spun in a small, tight circle, and she grabbed hold of his shoulders and let out a breathless gasp.

An odd mixture of delight and shock laced her

nervous laughter. "What has gotten in to you?" she whispered as her toes touched the floor. "Let me go. Customers are looking."

He grinned, his deep blue eyes twinkling with merriment. "Don't be so paranoid. No one's looking."

She glanced to her left. Sure enough, Al and Lyle were staring, one smirking, the other nodding as if to say, "*Oh, yeah. We'll be talking about this for the rest of the week.*"

Brad gently captured her jaw between his thumb and index finger and guided her face and her gaze to his.

"The winds, they are a changing." He breathed the words for her ears only.

For a split second, the intensity in his eyes, the silky feel of his warm breath against her cheek, mesmerized her. Then the cryptic message seeped into her brain and caused her brow to wrinkle. "Are you okay? You didn't get hit in the head with a surf board this morning, did you?"

Rather than answer her question, he just laughed, turned on his heel, snatched up his thermos from the counter, and made his way over to the drink station. As he unscrewed the lid, he swiveled his head to look at her.

"You're still going to participate in the lunch auction, right?" he asked her. "Plans are coming together and I need to get the list of participants to the printer so the programs will be ready for auction night. The whole team has been handing out fliers. And the newspapers have already started on publicity. Have you seen the ads? They turned out great."

Cathy automatically picked up the dish towel from the counter. "No one is going to bid on me, Brad. Who would pay to have lunch with me?"

"I'll bid," Al called out, raising his hand and waving.

"Me, too," Lyle chimed in. "Especially if Cathy's providing the lunch."

Al snickered. "You got that straight."

She shot the men a look.

"What?" Lyle said. "Come on, Cathy. It's a great cause. And you're a great cook."

While looking at Cathy, Al pointed a thumb at Lyle. "The man might not be a genius, but you can't argue with that kind of logic."

The proceeds of the fund raiser Brad had been

busy organizing for the past few weeks would go toward the ever-mounting medical costs of a local child who had been diagnosed with brain cancer. The hospital bills had nearly forced little Ethan Ferguson's parents into bankruptcy. The town residents had gathered at a council meeting back in the spring to discuss what could be done. The Ocean City Beach Patrol decided to auction off lunch with some of the guards as well as some prominent citizens: a couple of the town council members and a dozen or so business owners would be participating.

Steam wafted from Brad's thermos as he moseyed back toward the counter. "They're both right. On all counts. Come on, Cathy. What do you say?"

Before she could answer, he told her, "Heather's going to be there. Daniel said he'd bid whatever it took to win lunch with her." His tone lowered as he said, "Who knows? Maybe you and Heather might get a chance to talk at the auction."

As incentives went, that one wasn't all that great. The last thing Cathy wanted was for Heather to blow up on her and make a scene in front of a crowd of people. Not that she would expect Heather to do such a thing, but...

Brad's tawny brows went flat and his expression drooped like a hound dog begging for a biscuit. "Come on. Please?"

She sighed. "Okay. All right. I'll do it."

Al drummed a happy tune on the counter with his fingers, and Lyle said, "Yes! I'm going to win that lunch!"

"Oh, no," Al said. "I don't think so."

Lyle shook his head. "Then you don't think so good, my friend."

Brad beamed at Cathy as the men continued to bicker like magpies. "Thanks, Cath. I appreciate it. You won't regret it. I promise you." He bent close enough to kiss her cheek.

He smelled like sunshine and ocean waves, and Cathy dragged the scent of him deep into her lungs.

"I already regret it," she smirked. "You sure as hell better bid on me."

He chuckled. "Don't you worry about that. Now, I gotta run. I'm going to pop over and ask Sara to participate."

Cathy drew her chin back. "But she's eight months pregnant."

"So?" Brad screwed the lid onto his thermos. "That's just extra incentive for Landon to bid on his beautiful woman."

"Brad." Cathy couldn't keep the scoffing out of her tone. "Why don't you just ask them for a donation? That would be so much easier."

He smiled and his straight, white teeth gleamed. "Easier, maybe. But the competition will be much more fun." Then the amusement left his tone as he asked, "Hey, are you free for dinner tonight?"

The energy in his whole countenance changed. There was a depth in his blue gaze that stirred a need deep in the pit of her belly. Like warm, gray smoke, emotion curled and tightened her insides. Judging from the look he gave her, he was talking about much more than dinner.

"Yes," she said, her mouth suddenly dry with anticipation, "I'm free."

"Great. I'll call you later."

He hitched his backpack higher onto his shoulder and headed for the door, calling out for everyone in the café to have a good day.

* * *

Brad smiled in the darkness as he stared up at the ceiling. He liked the feel of cool, cotton sheets on his naked skin. He felt sated, satisfied, and he knew without a doubt that Cathy felt the same. Her breathing had gone slow and rhythmic, and he suspected she'd fallen asleep.

They'd had a good night. A *great* night. From start to finish.

The scallops and risotto at Liquid Assets had been delectable. The slice of Smith Island cake they'd shared, his favorite dessert, had been slathered with rich fudge frosting. They'd talked about their day and had ended up laughing.

He told her about a group of inquisitive kids he'd met who had asked him all manner of questions about his job and the seashore. How many people had he saved? Could he breathe underwater? Had he ever gotten caught in a rip current? Were there crocodiles in the ocean? Did dolphins eat people? Did he like to build sand castles? Had he ever been blown away by a hurricane? Did crabs have eyebrows? Were there more fish in the ocean than there were grains of sand?

Her day had been packed with staff issues, cooking for customers, and listening to Al and Lyle bicker over who would bid the most at the auction and win the right to have lunch with her. Apparently, the guys had concocted a scheme where, if the need arose, they would pool their money for a two-for-one deal, and the rest of their afternoon had been spent planning the menu for the anticipated lunch date. Cathy complained about the crusty oldsters, but Brad knew that the men held a special place in her heart.

He rolled over onto his side, raising his arm, and resting his jaw on his closed fist so he could look at her. Her skin glowed in the moonlight. She often lamented the fact that her skin refused to tan and claimed that, when it came to the sun, she had two colors—white and red. But he loved her porcelain-pale skin; it brought to mind fresh cream, and he fought the urge to lean forward and lick her sweet, naked flesh.

Her back was only partially to him, and propped up like he was, he let his eyes devour the swell of her breast beneath the sheet. Her dusky nipple protruded to a pert point and desire stirred in him. Her chest rose and fell in a peaceful cadence.

All through dinner, Brad had looked for a lull in the conversation during which he could tell her about his amazing stroke of luck. He was so excited about having inherited the mini golf course and arcade. A short-handed staff meant he'd spent the day in a guard chair, keeping watch over the swimmers, but he'd been glad to have the time to sit quietly and dream about the possibilities for the future.

The white cotton sheet covered the gentle curves of Cathy's waist and hip, but the fabric bunched high on her thigh, leaving her long, shapely legs open to his gaze. She had perfect calves, narrow ankles, even her feet were cute. Dark scarlet polish coated her toenails.

He hadn't found an opportune time to tell her about his good fortune. Not at dinner. Not at the pier where they'd gone to watch the sun go down. And not during the drive back to her house. Once there, he had become so lost in kissing her, touching her, slipping her clothes off, the whole idea of telling her had disappeared from his mind. Who could blame him for that?

Still... why hadn't he found a chance to tell her?

They'd been together for hours, and more than one opportunity had presented itself.

He shifted on the bed, tugged the sheet off his body, and stood up.

Was he really that leery of her reaction?

He found his trousers on the floor and quietly slid into them.

Maybe it would be best to clean the place up a bit first. Schedule a visit from the landscaper. The grass was knee-high in places. And he should probably find a carpenter and an electrician to give the golf course obstacles a good once-over to make sure all the moving parts were working. The indoor arcade games were in need of good cleaning; months of sitting idle had allowed a thick coat of gray dust to settle on everything.

Brad buttoned up his shirt and slid into his canvas Docksiders at the same time.

He wanted Cathy to be wowed. He wanted her to look around and see the successful business he intended to make of it. The place wasn't very impressive in its current state. Once he got it cleaned up, he could tell her.

The job shouldn't take long. As long as he arrived at the arcade early, he could get the crew started on their assignments each day before going to his ten o'clock beach patrol shift each morning. Dividing his time like this would be hectic, but he could handle it.

"Hey," she softly called from the bed. "You headed home?"

He nodded as he tucked his wallet into his back pocket and picked up his keys. The dark doubt that had seeped into the satisfied happiness he'd felt disturbed him.

"Yeah," he whispered. "I've got to be up early." He rounded the bed and kissed her gently on the forehead. "Stay put. I'll lock the door on my way out."

She murmured a thank you, then closed her eyes and drifted back to sleep. It was a sight he saw fairly often, one that never failed to conjure a warm smile. But an odd frown marred his brow as he left the bedroom and made his way to the front door.

CHAPTER THREE

Quiet enveloped the inside of the café like a piece of cotton batting, muffling the sounds coming from beyond the front door: the conversations and laughter of the people strolling along the boardwalk, the squeals of happy children, and the ever-present background noise of the ocean waves. She'd locked the door at two thirty that afternoon and hoped the last few customers would finish up their meals by three so she could hit the beach by four. Her staff had been quick and efficient in taking care of the end-of-shift tasks. Every table had been cleaned, the chairs had been perched upside down on the tabletops, the floor had been swept and mopped, the counter wiped down, and all the dishes and utensils had been washed, sterilized, and put away. The dining room and kitchen gleamed. She was ready for tomorrow morning's opening.

Slipping into her office and closing the door, she changed out of her work clothes and put on her bikini. She carefully coated every inch of her skin with sunscreen, put on her beach cover-up, and then went to the closet to pull out her umbrella, a chair, and her trusty tote that held a few cooking magazines she'd been eager to read.

Snagging her phone off her desk, she started tapping out a text to Brad, but then she paused before she'd completed the invitation to join her when he got off work.

Something was up with him, although she wasn't sure what. The last time they'd been together, he'd been so considerate, so... giving. Cathy grinned when she thought about just *how* giving he'd been. However, over the course of the following four days, she'd reached out to him a couple of times and he'd blown her off with vague excuses. That's how her relationship was with Brad; when he was with her, he could be so attentive that she felt like the only woman alive. But once they were apart, she seemed to easily slip his mind. That was okay. Really. She knew where she stood with the man.

Cathy decided to delete the text, and she sent one to Sara instead.

Cathy: Headed out to the beach. Want to join me?

Sara: Yes! Need some sunshine on my skin.

Sara: Just finishing up at the shop. Give me 15.

Cathy: No prob. Take ur time. Will bring a chair for u.

Sara: Thx.

Cathy: Head due east. :)

Sara: Will do.

Out on the beach, Cathy rocked the umbrella pole back and forth, forcing it into the sand. She caught sight of Heather on the front porch of the Lonely Loon with Daniel's little girl, Mia. With the umbrella open and secure, Cathy moved her tote next to the pole and positioned the chairs in the circle of shade. She tried not to glance toward the B&B but failed. On her second quick look, she spied Mia crossing the boardwalk. The child trudged toward her across the sand.

"Hey, sweet stuff." Cathy smiled broadly at Mia.

"I asked Heather if we could come say hi." Mia lifted her hand to shield her eyes from the sun. "She said she didn't want to get sand in her shoes. But she let me come by myself."

"I'm so glad you did." Cathy sat down and pointed to the empty chair. "Want to sit while we visit?"

"Okay." Mia's tone wavered a bit and she didn't move immediately toward the beach chair; instead, she darted a nervous glance back toward Heather.

Cathy was actually surprised that the child had come so far from the B&B all by herself. The ordeal Mia had experienced back in the winter had left her frightened and uncertain. Daniel had taken his daughter to visit family in some Eastern European country, and his deceased wife's sister had snatched the child and had kept her from Daniel for many long, agonizing weeks.

"You're safe, sweetheart," Cathy assured her

softly. "Heather will stand right there on the porch until you get back, I'm sure of it."

Mia nodded and then sat down in the shade of the umbrella.

"You haven't been to the café for breakfast for a while," Cathy said. "I've missed you."

"I've been helping Heather. She keeps me awful busy."

Cathy chuckled. "I'm sure. Running a bed and breakfast is hard work. And this is the busiest part of the season."

Mia agreed with an exaggerated nod of her head. Her big eyes went round. "And those people... they really like to *talk*."

"Yes, they do." Cathy reined in the humor tugging at the corners of her mouth.

"I got a kitten," Mia pronounced.

"You did?"

"I'm really happy." The little girl's words were breathed on a sigh. "I wasn't sure it was going to happen. Heather was worried the people who come to stay with us might be lergic to cats."

"*Allergic?*"

"Yeah, lergic." Mia's dark head bobbed enthusiastically. "That means Midnight might make 'em sneeze and make their nose run with snot. Daddy told me snot is mucus, and it's sticky like flypaper. To catch the stuff you don't want to breath in. And then there are the hives. Big, red blotches. Heather told me about those."

Cathy flattened her lips for a moment. Not only had her correction in word pronunciation been completely lost on Mia, the child's overly detailed description of what it meant to have allergies made Cathy want to howl with laughter.

"At dinner one night," Mia explained, "we decided I couldn't have a kitten. But then the next day Heather and Daddy changed their minds and we went to pick up Midnight at the animal place. I think it was called the Human Society."

"The *Humane* Society," Cathy corrected. After she wrangled her funny bone under control, she remarked, "Midnight is a nice name for a kitten."

"Yeah. She's black all over. She's so soft. And pretty, too." Mia shifted on the beach chair. "You should come see her. I'll hold her while you pet her. She won't scratch you. She's really, *really* nice."

"I'm sure she's very nice." Cathy's voice went soft and hesitant as she pondered the child's invitation.

Mia's little chin tipped up. "Will you come see her?"

"Well, honey... you see..." Her voice trailed off.

"Are you lergic to cats?"

"No. Honey, that's not it."

A tiny wrinkle creased Mia's forehead. "Cathy, are you and Heather lergic to each other?"

The unexpected question made Cathy's mouth form a small "oh" and she blinked rapidly several times.

"Sara keeps telling me that you and Sara and Heather are friends," Mia said. "Sara comes to visit us almost every day. She brings muffins and rolls and cakes and stuff for breakfast, and she always spends some time talking in the kitchen. But you never come. And when I asked Heather about it, her nose squinched up like she was about to sneeze." The little girl pointed at Cathy's face. "Just like yours just did when I asked you to come see Midnight."

Cathy let her shoulders relax and she inhaled a slow, deep breath. My, oh, my, this child had beaucoup powers of perception. If she was this sharp at five years old, what would she be like as a teen? Daniel and Heather were in for some trouble.

"No, sweetheart, Heather and I aren't allergic to each other." Cathy smiled, deciding quickly to steer clear of any more mention of her and Heather's problems. "But I do have an idea. Why don't you bring your new kitten to the café tomorrow morning? I'll cook you a big stack of blueberry pancakes, and while you eat them at my desk, I'll visit with Midnight in my office."

Mia's whole body perked up. "Yeah, that sounds like fun. I guess you can't have a kitten in the kitchen, huh." Then her little mouth pursed. "I have to ask Daddy and Heather first."

"Of course, you do."

She pushed herself out of the chair and stepped out into the sunshine. "I'd better go. I need to check on Midnight."

Cathy nodded. "Thanks for the visit. If you can't come tomorrow, it's okay."

"I'm pretty sure Daddy will say yes." Mia grinned, her voice lowering. "When I talk fast and say please lots of times, he usually says yes."

"I'm sure he does," Cathy murmured under her breath.

And with a wave, Mia kicked sand as she sprinted back toward the boardwalk and Heather, who continued to stand sentinel on the porch. During the half minute or so that it took Mia to make the short journey, Heather never acknowledged Cathy. Narrowing her eyes and screwing up her mouth, Cathy whipped out her phone and tapped a text message.

Cathy: You should forgive me.
Cathy: You know about global warming, right?
Cathy: The sun could scorch me to death.

She shot her gaze toward Heather, saw her friend pause and reach into her pocket for her cell phone. Mia was talking to Heather as she climbed the front steps of the B&B. Heather took the little girl's hand and led her toward the front door. Once Mia disappeared inside, Heather paused at the threshold. Cathy felt a little giddy, knowing the texts she sent were being read. She watched closely for some reaction.

Heather held her phone in both hands. Cathy's heart fluttered. Was Heather actually sending her a response?

Cathy's phone trilled. Breathlessly, she looked at the screen.

would follow. And they had, like starving hawks stalking rabbits.

The music and dinging and buzzing of the electronic machines, the murmuring, laughing crowd, the clacking of the skee ball lanes were enough to cover Cathy's irate shouting. The boys just laughed, and when she'd continued to berate them, their belligerence had turned to anger. When Ronny dipped his chin and came toward her, Cathy hadn't thought; she'd merely reacted. She'd clenched her fist and swung as hard as she could. She struck him square in the nose, knocking him off his feet. Blood had spurted like a geyser. In an instant, his mouth and chin became a slick, sickening red. Blood stained his t-shirt, smeared her hand, dotted her pretty blue top and arms.

Horror and pain widened the boy's gaze, and his hands flew to his face. Shock made Andrew go silent. Cathy glanced back at Heather, whose face had been frozen in abject horror.

Cathy remembered standing there for what felt like several drawn-out seconds, confused about what she should be feeling. Should she be unnerved by her actions? Afraid of the consequences? In the end, all she felt was mad.

After he'd scrambled to his feet, she'd stepped up to him, her nose so close to his chin she could smell the metallic scent of his blood, and she'd growled, "You tell anyone about this, and I'll make sure everybody at school knows a girl made you bleed." She'd barked at Heather and Sara to follow her, and she hadn't looked back as she'd stormed out of the arcade and into the bright sunshine.

There had been several times Cathy had utilized violence as a kid to solve her problems. She shifted on the beach chair uneasily, wondering if her adolescent tendency toward physical force had anything to do with her nightmare of a marriage.

No. She wasn't going to that dark place. Not today.

Cathy took a slow, deep breath and gazed out at the blue green ocean. The water undulated, glistening in the sunshine. The iridescent sparkle calmed her.

Heather had been the impetus of this particular reminiscence. Heather and her mule-like stubbornness. After the bloody incident in the arcade, Heather hadn't spoken to Ronny or Andrew again. Ever. All through their school years, it had been as though the boys were dead to her. Heather's bullheadedness could be as rigid as a steel I-beam.

The fact that Heather had responded to the text was a good sign. A very good sign.

"What are you grinning about?" Sara dipped her head as she stepped under the umbrella.

"Heather," Cathy admitted breezily. She automatically stood up and helped Sara ease her pregnant body down into the beach chair.

Once settled, Sara murmured her thanks. "What are you saying? Heather's talked to you? She's forgiven you?"

"No. Not yet. But she did call me the Wicked Witch of the West."

"Ah. Now *that's* something to get excited about." Sarcasm bit deeply into Sara's words.

"Don't you see?" Cathy's grin widened. "I'm wearing her down."

"Um-hm. I can see that." Sara moistened her lips and added, "Like water on rock."

A hot summer breeze stirred the salty air. Several gulls hovered on the wind, and then dive-bombed to the sand to squabble over a few potato chips that had been dropped by some children. One toddler pointed at the birds, calling to his mother to look, and as his head was turned, one wily seagull swooped in and snatched the chip right out of his fingers. The child started in fear, and for a moment it looked as though he might cry. But he laughed and raced to the blanket where his mother lay, sunning herself.

"So what's going on?" Cathy asked Sara. "How are you feeling?"

"I'm just disgusted with myself. I can't figure out if I'm annoyed with Landon, or if I just want to get this pregnancy over with." She sighed. "I'm tired of looking like a whale. I'm hot and sweaty all the time. And it was stupid to plan a baby's arrival right in the middle of tourist season."

The sand felt warm against the back of Cathy's heel as she dug a furrow. "You planned the baby's arrival?"

Sara narrowed her eyes. "Shut up."

Cathy laughed. "Okay, back up a second. Why are you upset with Landon? What could that man possibly have done to—"

"Look, just because he fixed the plumbing," Sara said, "doesn't make him some kind of hero. He can be annoying."

Since Landon's arrival last year, there had been

far fewer drips and leaks and outright floods caused by the ancient plumbing system in the building that housed their businesses. In Cathy's opinion, that made the man a superstar.

"You are really cranky," Cathy said. "What is up with you?"

Sara heaved a sigh, swiping her palm across her big, baby-filled belly. "It's that stupid wedding."

"Stupid?" When her friend's eyes welled with tears, Cathy sat up a little straighter. "Honey, what is it? Talk to me."

"I don't think Landon wants the wedding."

Bending forward, Cathy reached out and slid her hand over Sara's forearm. "Sara, Landon loves you. He's ecstatic about the baby. Of course, he wants to get married."

Sara sniffed and swiped at an errant tear. "No, that's not what I mean. He wants to get married. But—" she paused long enough to swallow back her emotion "—he mentioned this morning that we should just go to the courthouse and *get it over with*. Those are his exact words, Cathy. *Get it over with*."

Not being a huge champion of the institution of marriage, herself, Cathy didn't view Landon's suggestion as all that outlandish. But seeing how the idea distressed Sara, Cathy kept her thoughts to herself.

"It's his sister," Sara said. "I know it is."

"He still hasn't talked to her?"

Cathy knew Landon and his sister, who lived in Kansas with her husband and two children, had been on the outs since before Landon had arrived in Ocean City.

"They've exchanged a couple of phone calls." Sara rummaged in her tote bag and then she put on a pair of sunglasses. "But their conversations have been too short for them to say anything meaningful, or to work out anything. And then he spends two or three days acting like he's in a huff." Sara flicked another tear from her cheek. "How hard can it be? She's his sister, for cryin' out loud. He ought to be able to tell her how he feels."

All Cathy could think about was her trouble with Heather. Sure, they weren't blood relatives, but they were closer than sisters. It would seem that talking out your differences should be easy.

But it wasn't, now, was it?

"For about fifteen minutes today," Sara said, "I considered taking him up on it. Just grabbing him by the shirt collar and getting in his truck and driving to the county courthouse. I thought, let's just *get it over with*." The breeze fluttered her bangs. "But then I thought about Mom. She'd be heartbroken, Cathy. She's spent so much time and effort making plans for the ceremony."

Cathy tilted her head to the side. Sara must feel hemmed in... caught between two people she loves.

"Mom hasn't been feeling well," Sara admitted. "Her pain is getting steadily worse. And focusing on the wedding plans has been a good diversion for her. She's gone into meticulous detail."

Geneva had been battling spinal stenosis since she took a fall. That must have been twenty five years ago. That's a long time to be living with pain. Some days were so bad the poor woman couldn't get out of bed.

"Sara, I want you to listen to me." Cathy sat up straight. "You shouldn't be feeling this kind of stress. You need to think about the baby. You need to relax. Take it easy. I mean it."

The sigh Sara heaved seemed soul deep.

"I feel caught between doing what Landon wants to do," she told Cathy, "and doing what Mom wants to do."

Cathy's tone softened as she asked, "What do *you* want to do?"

Emotion glistened in Sara's suddenly moist gaze. "I don't know. I'm just so tired."

Going still, Cathy battled her knee-jerk reaction. She wanted to hug her friend tightly. She also wanted to call both Landon and Geneva and give them hell for what they were doing to Sara. But knowing her friend, Cathy figured Sara probably hadn't even told Landon or Geneva about the pressure she was experiencing. And if Cathy were to reach out to Sara right now, they'd both end up in tears.

"Well, you don't have to do anything until after the baby is born." Cathy combed her hair out of her face with her fingers. "Hell, you don't have to do anything, for that matter. Who says you have to get married, anyway?"

The sound of Sara's chuckle lifted Cathy's worry a bit.

"Figures you'd say that."

Now Cathy laughed. "Does figure, doesn't it? But it's true."

Sara changed the subject altogether. "Hey, what's Brad up to now?"

"What do you mean?"

"He's meeting with Landon today," Sara said. "I think he's going to offer Landon some work."

"Oh?" Cathy shrugged one shoulder. "Maybe he needs stages made for the lunch auction. It's coming up soon."

Sara shook her head, shoving her sunglass up onto her nose. "No, Landon finished that job last week. This is something else. Something personal. A new business, maybe? I went to help Mom get dressed this morning, so I wasn't able to ask before Landon left the house."

Again, Cathy shrugged. "You got me."

The little boy with the potato chips squealed as he chased a seagull, and both women cast a quick glance his way.

"Brad lives on a lifeguard salary," Cathy murmured. "The man barely has two nickels to rub together. I can't see him starting a business."

"I'll see what I can find out," Sara said. "And I'll give you a call."

"Nah." Cathy waved her hand in the air. "Don't bother. If Brad wants me to know what he's doing, he'll tell me."

But curiosity had her inside tingling. Maybe

Brad hadn't been avoiding her because he'd found a tempting tourist to spend time with this week. Maybe his absence was due to something else entirely.

CHAPTER FOUR

His fingertips blazed a slow, erotic trail over her shoulder and down her arm. He slid the palm of his other hand up the flat of her stomach. Cathy's breath caught and her blood seemed to chug through her body.

The cologne he wore set off a chain of olfactory sensations that triggered an intense desire in her. A hint of leather mingled with the rich scent of cedar, and there was a distinctive top note of some exotic oriental flower. Bergamot, maybe?

Whatever it was, the alluring smell had her pressing her nose to his chest.

She kissed his heated skin and then tipped up her chin and laved his dark nipple with a gentle lick of her tongue. Brad's breathy groan made Cathy smile lazily. She loved that she could provoke such a sexy reaction from him.

He pushed her onto her back and rolled on top of her, lacing his fingers with hers, and sliding their hands up, up, up toward the bed's headboard. He kissed her then, slowly, deeply, and her pulse thudded between her legs like a fiery drum beat. His lips roved over her jaw, her neck, her breasts, and she heard a tiny, desperate mewing sound and knew it came from her own throat. She needed him so badly she thought she would lose her mind from the wanting.

He nudged her legs further apart with his knees, and she gladly opened herself to him. As he slid into her, he covered her mouth with his. Every sense burst to life, and release came after just a few full, deep thrusts.

Cathy was still panting out contented sighs when he slid off her and rolled out of bed. She dragged her eyes open, shoving her sweat-damped hair from her face. The corded muscles of his back played beneath his golden skin. His luscious glutes tightened as he bent at the waist and shoved one foot into a heavy rubber boot.

Her gaze narrowed and confusion buzzed in her head like a swarm of paper wasps.

Why was he wearing fireman's boots?

Brad snatched up a towel and tucked it around his waist.

"Sorry," he told her. "Gotta run. There's a tempting tourist waiting for me at Seacrets."

Hot tears rushed to her eyes, scorching her eye sockets. Jealousy and resentment walloped her with the force of a well-aimed baseball bat...

And she gasped her way out of the dream turned nightmare.

"What the hell?" She blinked in the darkness, and once she realized she was alone, she huffed out a breath meant to dispel the emotion and the achy need that tensed every muscle in her body.

She kicked and shoved her way out of the tangle of top sheet and blanket to sit on the edge of the mattress. A dull remnant of lust continued to pulse low in her abdomen.

Why on earth had her subconscious conjured

that dream? For sexual release, sure. That was understandable. But what was up with those fireman's boots? And Brad's comment about the tempting tourist... and those overwhelming feelings of—

Cathy shook her head and stood up.

The glowing numbers on the clock told her she had another hour to sleep, but she sure as heck wasn't interested in trying. Taking a deep breath, she headed to the bathroom.

What a way to start the day.

* * *

Maple syrup dribbled down Mia's chin and plopped on the top of Cathy's desk. The little girl had arrived at the back door of the kitchen in her pajamas and fuzzy slippers with the coal black kitten tucked securely under her arm, saying her daddy told her if she wanted to bring Midnight for a visit she had to do it before the customers arrived. Cathy whipped up a batch of silver dollar blueberry pancakes and then the two of them went into the office to keep the cat away from the cooking area.

"She's so soft." Cathy made kissy noises and Midnight mewed. Like every other animal, this one loved to be scratched behind the ears.

"She's my favoritest thing in the whole wide world," Mia said. She wiped her mouth on her bare arm.

"There's a napkin there," Cathy reminded her.

Mia promptly picked up the napkin, dabbed at her already clean lips, and picked up her fork. "These pancakes are really delicious. Blueberries are my very favorite."

Cathy smiled. "Mine, too."

In the silent seconds that followed, Cathy cradled Midnight and wiggled her fingers several inches above the animal's front paws, enticing her to play. The kitten watched for a moment and then batted at Cathy's hand.

"Are you comin' to the baby party?"

Mia's question came out of the blue.

"The baby party?" Cathy went still, her voice softening as she repeated the phrase.

Sara's baby shower. Heather was planning the shower.

Several emotions welled up in her at the same time—annoyance, frustration, sadness. She should be helping with the plans. She was Sara's friend, too. But causing a ruckus would only cause Sara more stress than she was already under. Heather was obviously still plenty angry, and that's why she was making plans on her own, Cathy guessed.

She could poke, prod, and vex with those smartass texts she'd been sending, but until Heather decided to forgive her, there was really nothing substantive Cathy could do except wait it out.

Patience wasn't a virtue Cathy possessed.

Mia's beautiful dark eyes went round. "Did you know Sara has a baby in her tummy?"

Thankfully, before Cathy could respond, Mia continued.

"I'm not sure how it got in there." The child's brow wrinkled. "I asked Daddy and he 'splained it." She shook her head. "But I'm still confused."

Please don't ask me any questions! Please. Please. Please! The thought ricocheted through her brain like a ping pong ball that had been given a hefty swat. That's all she needed; Heather's already heated anger being further fueled by some misstatement Cathy made to Mia about the birds and the bees.

Without thought, Mia dropped her fork, twisted her wrist, and licked a blob of buttery syrup off the fleshy part of her hand. Then she looked up at Cathy.

"You don't know either, huh?" Mia picked up the napkin and rubbed at the sticky spot on her hand. Her mouth screwed up as though she were in deep thought. Softly, she asked, "How'd that baby get... *in* there?"

Cathy picked up Midnight in one hand and stroked the kitten's back with the other. Casually, she said, "I'm sure if you ask your dad he'll be happy to explain it all again."

She seriously doubted Daniel would be happy about it. But that wasn't Cathy's concern. She'd clearly overstepped the bounds when she'd told Daniel about Heather's most vulnerable secret, but Cathy had no problem whatsoever steering clear of the how-do-babies-get-in-there conversation.

She wasn't going there. Nope.

The sound of keys tapping on the front door had her thanking her lucky stars. She leaned forward and peered out her office door. Al and Lyle stood in the yellowy gleam of the outside light.

Cathy stood up. "I'd better get that. There are

hungry people at the door. Time to open up the café."

Those ornery, *lovely* men! There was a free cup of coffee in their very near future due to their serendipitous arrival.

Mia immediately climbed down from the desk chair. "I gotta go," she said as she rounded the desk. She scooped Midnight out of Cathy's hand. "Daddy said I need to come home as soon as customers start coming."

Relief flooded Cathy and she released a pent up breath. What a wonderful, obedient child. She grinned.

Just a few minutes later, Cathy poured coffee into mugs for Al and Lyle. She had escorted Mia and Midnight out the back door into the hallway and watched the little girl trek up the stairs that led to The Lonely Loon. The relief she felt over having avoided more of Mia's questions continued to make her smile.

"Here you go, gentleman," she nearly sang the words. "Coffee's on the house this morning."

Al looked pleasantly surprised and automatically reached for the cream pitcher. Lyle, on the other hand, frowned as he leaned away from the counter.

"What's going on?" he asked Cathy. "You don't give away free coffee. Is this left over from yesterday?"

"Lyle, quit examining the horse's teeth," Al warned.

The other man scowled. "What the hell is that supposed to mean?"

Al sighed. "You know. The gift horse? You don't look in its mouth?"

Lyle waved him off grumpily. "Bah."

"It's a fresh pot, Lyle," Cathy assured him. "Hot and strong."

"I'd say that's exactly what he needs," Al murmured, "to draw out his sunny disposition."

She chuckled as she plunked two blueberry muffins onto plates and set them down in front of them. "On the house."

"Okay." Al leaned back, arching his brows and nodding at Lyle. "I agree with you now. Something really is up with her."

"Maybe she's afraid no one is going to bid on her for the lunch auction," Lyle surmised.

Al swiveled his head to look at Cathy. "But we already told you we would pool our cash."

"It has nothing to do with the auction." Cathy went to put the lid back on the muffins. "You two saved me from an awkward conversation with Mia. She's wondering how that baby got into Sara's tummy."

Instantly, both men understood the reason for Cathy's gratitude.

"I hope you sent her back upstairs to Heather and her dad," Al said as he stuck his spoon in his mug and stirred.

"That's *exactly* what I did."

The three of them were still laughing and joking about the kiddy-talk pitfalls she had barely avoided when the wait staff arrived, and Cathy slipped into her office with them to dole out the day's table assignments.

Soon customers filled the café. Bacon, sausage patties, and ham sizzled on the wide surface of the screaming hot grill along with eggs, pancakes, and hash browns.

She had just plated three lemon ricotta pancakes, a new recipe she was trying out on the menu, when she overheard Lyle let out a long-winded whistle.

"He must be mortgaged up the eyeballs," he told Al.

Cathy added three sausage patties to the plate and walked the order to the counter. "Order's up!" she called. Then curiosity drew her over to the men sitting at the counter.

"Who are you gossiping about today?" she asked them.

"Brad," Al said. "The clerk over at Town Hall told me he's the new owner of the arcade on Stargrass Avenue."

Lyle tapped the counter with his spoon. "That place takes up a whole block. Must be worth a cool million."

"Or more," Al added.

"No way." Cathy scoffed. "He doesn't have that kind of money. And he doesn't have collateral for that kind of loan." She shook her head hard enough to set her pony tail swinging as she repeated, "No way."

Al lifted his shoulders and hands, palm up, in an exaggerated shrug. "I'm just telling you what I heard."

Three orders came in right on top of each other, and Cathy had to scurry back into the kitchen. She added another half pound of bacon to the grill and poured out three portions of pancake batter, then slid a baking pan covered with biscuits into the oven, all the while feeling a tense consternation knitting her brow.

Either the clerk had given Al some bad information, or Brad was getting himself into some deep doo-doo.

CHAPTER FIVE

T he noise of the shop-vac blared in Brad's left ear. He shifted the dust mask to cover his nose and then stuck his whole upper body, along with the vacuum's hose, into the now-empty display cabinet. Dust, bits of paper, and years of accumulated grunge disappeared into the nozzle. He could hear the debris pinging its way through the hose as it was sucked from every surface, corner, and crevice. It was clear the place hadn't been very well maintained, and having sat empty and unused hadn't helped.

Once it was clean, the cabinet would display various toys, from small plastic doodads to more elaborate prizes, that kids could choose from in exchange for the coupon tickets spit out by the coin-operated game machines. Brad remembered, as a kid, spending hours playing pinball machines or Donkey Kong or Pac-Man, and then saving up his tickets, sometimes for weeks, just so he could have that one perfect prize.

Looking up through the hazy glass shelf, he noted that one of the light bulbs in the roof of the cabinet needed replacing and he made a mental note to buy bulbs at the hardware store. Dirt and dust were his main enemies at the moment; every surface inside the arcade had been covered in a gray film. He'd hired a small crew, and slowly but surely, the place was being scrubbed down, worked over, and oiled up so he could open before the season ended.

Jack had been a godsend. While Brad was busy with life guard duties during daylight hours, Jack had been helping to supervise the cleaning crew by popping in several times a day to keep them on track. Luckily, Brad had found most all of the arcade games in working order once he'd had the electricity turned on, and he had Landon working on the machines in need of repair which included two skee ball lanes and one of the animated dinosaurs outside on the mini golf course.

The light tap on the front of the display case had him gazing up through the glass. Jack motioned to him, pointing toward the front door as he mouthed the word *visitor*. Brad pulled his upper body from the close confines of the cabinet and flipped off the shop-vac.

He looked toward the front of the building and saw that Cathy had stopped near the row of skee ball lanes to talk to Landon. She laughed at something he said, and then Cathy swiveled her head, her gaze latching onto Brad, her perfectly arched eyebrows lifting just a fraction.

He felt like an alley cat caught hacking out yellow feathers, and he had no idea why. Well, that wasn't quite true. He felt guilty that he hadn't told her about the arcade himself. Evidently, she'd learned about it from someone else. Cathy sauntered toward him, her Bermuda shorts and next-to-nothing sandals showing off the lean muscles of her sexy calves. She stopped and smiled.

"Hey there, Jack," she greeted.

His friend nodded. "How are you, Cathy?"

"Fine," she quipped. "You?"

"Good," Jack said. "Real good."

She turned her attention to Brad, her smile never wavering as she stood on one side of the waist-high display cabinet and he stood on the other. Despite the odd feeling in his gut, the corners of his mouth drew back, curling into a smile.

Two or three awkward seconds ticked by, silent only in the fact that he and Cathy hadn't exchanged a greeting. The air around, however, was alive with a wild array of noise from pinball machines and other electronic games. Rock music rained down from the speakers in the rafters.

"Well," Jack told them, lifting the screwdriver he held in his hand, "I'm sure I could find more screws to tighten someplace. See you around, Cathy."

"See ya, Jack." Cathy's deep brown eyes continued to study Brad's face.

He rounded the cabinet and reached out to glide

his fingers along her bare upper arm. She felt good, looked good. Silky smooth and pale as moonlight.

"It's good to see you," he told her.

Her lids lowered in a slow blink and her lips compressed slightly, but she didn't resist when he leaned forward to kiss her cheek. Her strawberry blond hair smelled of coconut and almonds, and a spark of desire clenched in his belly.

He stepped back. "I want to hug you but I'm covered in dust." Without waiting for her to respond, he asked, "So who told you? How'd you find out?"

Her chuckle rippled over him like shallow waves of sun-warmed sea water.

"It's a small town, Brad. You know that."

"Yeah, I do."

"Nobody can keep a secret for long."

"I wasn't keeping a secret," he assured her. Then he looked out across the arcade. "I just wanted to get the place cleaned up a bit before I told you."

"Things do look a little run down."

He tamped down the insult welling in him and sighed. She was only speaking the truth.

"We're working on that."

"We?"

"Yeah," was all he said. But his hope that she'd leave it alone was quickly dashed.

"Well, I know Landon didn't go in on this venture with you," she said. "Sara would have told me. So this is something you cooked up with Jack? How long have you been thinking about going into business together?"

The curiosity she exhibited was normal, he guessed. As was her assumption of a business partner. He expected the same sort of questions from family and friends, once they discovered he owned the arcade. But something in her tone poked him like a blunt-tipped stick to the ribs.

"Jack has nothing to do with this," he said. "Well, other than helping me get the place ready to open. No, this is all me."

Her dark eyes widened just a fraction. A stranger might not have noticed, but he could read this woman. Like words on a page.

Before she could ask any more questions, he took her hand in his. "Come on. I want to show you something."

He tugged her along with him toward the north wall of the building. He shoved open the door of a long, narrow room, flipped on the light, and pulled her inside.

The cleaning crew hadn't touched this area. Cobwebs draped in the corners and dust floated in the air. Replacement parts for games sat on the counters lining the walls, a half dozen paint cans were stacked on the floor, plastic and metal containers were filled with nails and screws, nuts and bolts. This was clearly a workroom used to repair the machines, but Brad had other ideas.

"I'm going to turn this into a snack bar." He moved several feet into the room and opened his arms waist high. "I'll open this wall and put a counter here for seating." He turned a hundred and eighty degrees. "A small grill here for burgers and hot dogs. A deli fridge here to hold sandwich fixings. A deep fryer for French fries. A pizza oven back there, maybe."

"It's an awfully tight space."

She'd followed him further into the room.

"Once that wall is removed and the counter is installed, it'll feel bigger. More open. And there's a broom closet back there," he told her, indicating the wall opposite the door where they'd entered. "It'll give me at least six more feet of space."

"Well... maybe..." Doubt dulled the edges of her tone.

Dust and grime be damned. He turned to face her, wrapped his arms around her, and pulled her close. He kissed her mouth hard and then grinned down into her beautiful, surprised face.

"I'm excited about this, Cathy," he said.

The lines on her forehead softened and a hint of a smile toyed with her lips. She glanced down where their bodies were pressed together and then lifted her eyes to his.

"Believe me. I get that," she teased.

He laughed, stepping away from her. "I realize I have to get approval from the town. But I've got time. Once I get the paperwork sorted and I find the right construction crew, I figure the snack bar could be up and running come spring, don't you think?"

As he spoke, the flat of her hand made contact with the raw plywood counter, and she immediately pulled it back, her nose wrinkling. She swiped her palm off on the butt of her shorts.

"That sounds like a reasonable time frame to me."

"So do you think you could help me?"

Her dark gaze found his and he rushed to clarify.

"I'd like some help with the planning," he said. "What equipment should go where, the width of the counters, how large the refrigeration unit will need to be and the best place to put it. That kind of thing."

She licked her dusky lips.

"And next spring," he continued, "I'll need help staffing the place. I have no idea what makes a good short order cook. You could sit in on the interviews with me." He stopped long enough to swallow. "If you don't mind."

Finally, she said, "I don't mind."

Relief flooded through him and he wrapped her in a bear hug. The happiness that filled his chest made him want to dance around with her, but the narrow floor space made that impossible.

So, instead, he kissed her again.

Her soft lips tasted slightly sweet, as if she'd been nibbling on honey, and he wondered if it could be her lip balm or if it was just his imagination. Holding her in his arms bolstered his confidence. He could do this. He could pull it off. And he intended to do just that because, as he saw it, making this business a success was the only path to achieving his other, more personal plan.

"This could change everything for us," he whispered against her lips.

"I'm glad you like change."

The strength in her curt statement snuffed out the subtle alluring hint he'd tried to convey.

She shrugged out of his embrace, continuing to voice her thought. "Because a lot of change is going to have to take place if you want to get a snack bar up and running before next season."

He heaved a sigh, his arms feeling suddenly empty. He placed his hands on his hips and nodded as he looked around him. "You're right about that."

Her head tilted to the side. "So does this mean you're giving up your job as a life guard?"

"Not this season," he said. "I couldn't leave them in a lurch like that." He offered a small shrug. "I'll worry about next season later."

She was quiet for a moment. Then she said, "I'm starved. I was about to grab something to eat. You want to come?"

"I'd love to, but I have a few more things I want to do here. And then I have at least two dozen calls to make for Saturday's auction. You're still planning to be there, right?"

"I'll be there," she told him. She shifted the strap of her leather handbag on her shoulder and walked out the door.

Brad followed her, flipping off the light switch on his way out.

Suddenly, she turned to face him.

"Listen, do you think you could talk Landon into buying Sara some flowers?" she asked. "Or taking her out to dinner tonight? Something to make her feel special? She's been a little..." She paused before adding, "Stressed."

"She's going to have a baby," Brad said. "Her whole world is about to be turned upside down. It wouldn't be normal if she wasn't stressed."

Cathy shook her head. "It's more than just the baby. But I can't, you know..."

Brad nodded. "You can't rat on your friend?"

Her eyes widened and then she winced. "I did that once. And I'm still paying for it." She arched her brows at him. "Do you think you could help me help Sara?"

"I can do that. No problem."

"Thanks, Brad. You're a peach."

He watched her walk across the arcade, the gentle sway of her hips making him smile. If he got this right, he just might be able to make her his forever.

"So what did she say?"

Brad snapped his gaze around and saw Jack standing next to the air hockey table. "She's going to help me plan out the snack bar."

"That's good." Jack slid the screwdriver into his back pocket. "But what did she say?"

A perplexed frown bit into his brow.

"Was she happy about your good fortune?" Jack asked. "Your inheritance?"

When Brad didn't answer, it was Jack's turn to frown in bewilderment. "You did tell her, didn't you?"

Brad gazed off across the building, licked his lips, swallowed. Then he looked back at Jack. "No," he admitted. "I didn't tell her."

"I don't get it. Why the hell not?"

The conflicting thoughts that had been cluttering Brad's head since the day he'd learned of his windfall had him going quiet and he looked off toward the far side of the arcade. Through the large plate glass windows, he saw the colorful dinosaurs that decorated the mini golf course; a vibrant green velociraptor, a brick red stegosaurus, and in the distance, the head and neck of a magnificent gray brachiosaurus that towered over all the figures. For the most part, he'd been able to ignore the troubling disquiet that had seemed intent on infecting his brain. But not anymore. Not with Jack confronting him with such a pointed question.

He looked at Jack, his mouth drawing down as he slowly shook his head from side to side.

"I think," he began, "it's because, well, all this came too easily." He swung his hand in a small arc to indicate everything around him. "I'm still trying to wrap my own head around what this will mean. How this is going to change my life. How heavy this load might get."

Jack's gaze narrowed. "Load? You're talking like this might not be a good thing. It's like you won the freakin' lottery, man."

"I know. I know. And I realize it's a good thing. A great thing." He clamped his teeth down on his bottom lip for a second, then added, "It's just that it came, you know, out of the blue."

Jack laughed. "That's how good luck works. It thumps you right between the eyes. One second you're squeaky clean, and the next, the blue bird of happiness done pooped all over you. Abrupt change isn't always bad."

"I got that," he said. "I do. It's just that this inheritance thing..." The rest of his thought petered out as he sighed. "All this good fortune has started me thinking. I've had it so good, you know? I've had a good life. I was raised by two parents who love me. I grew up in a great place, had tons of friends. I was popular all through high school. I was well-liked. I breezed through college. I didn't have to struggle to find a job afterward. I've lived in the same house for, well, for forever. I have a real sense of security."

He paused for a beat. "I've lived a charmed life."

Confusion shadowed Jack's featured. "Okay," he said, drawing out the word.

"Cathy, on the other hand," Brad said, "didn't have it so easy. She never knew her father, and her mother died of a drug overdose when Cathy was almost too young to remember." His tone lowered as he added, "Almost."

Jack's chin lifted. "Wow. I had no idea."

"She was raised by her grandmother, a woman who was sour and strict and seemed hell-bent on keeping Cathy attached to her hip so she didn't follow in her mother's footsteps." Memories had Brad grimacing. "When Cathy and I dated back in high school, I can't tell you the elaborate stories we came up with just so she could get out of the house for a few hours. Nothing that would hurt anyone, mind you. She was just a normal teen wanting a little sip of freedom."

Shrugging, Jack grinned. "I told my share of white lies as a teen, believe me."

Brad nodded. Then he said, "Then Cathy's marriage went bad. And as soon as she came back to Ocean City, her grandmother got sick and ended up passing away."

"Damn," Jack said.

"Exactly."

His friend reached up and scrubbed at the back of his neck. "I guess all that crap is why Cathy's got such a... hard edge."

Brad tamped down the knee-jerk insult he felt on Cathy's behalf. "She's got a kind streak, too."

Jack looked dubious.

"You've been to the café, right?" Brad shifted his weight. "You know the two old guys who are always at the counter? Yeah, well, Cathy hooked them up. Al and Lyle were both widowers, pretty much lost in their grief. Cathy introduced them, and she puts up with their bickering and their grumpiness every day because, well, if she didn't they'd be all alone. She..."

He let the rest of the thought fade, brushing his palms together just so he'd have something to do with his hands. "Her tongue might be sharp, but she thinks about others, does things for people, out of the blue. I remember, years ago, my mom was battling a bad case of the flu, and Cathy brought her some homemade chicken noodle soup. She and I weren't dating at the time or anything. She'd just heard that my mom was sick, and there she was on our doorstep with this container of soup. My parents were amazed at her thoughtfulness." He shrugged. "So was I." Then his voice went soft. "But I never really appreciated the gesture until years later."

Jack rested a fist on his hip. "If she's as you say, kind and thoughtful, then..." He shook his head a little. "Why can't you tell her about your inheritance?"

He sighed. "I don't know really. For days now, I've been wondering why the hell life works out in such extremes for some people. In my case, all good. In Cathy's case, mostly bad. Shouldn't life be a balance? I mean, how am I supposed to tell her that some billionaire—who I never really knew—set me up so that I don't have to worry about money ever again? How unfair is that?"

Uneasiness fringed the sound of Jack's chuckle. "Look, I'm sorry Cathy's had it so tough," he said. "As much as I want to commiserate with you, I think you're making more of this than you should. I mean, seriously, look around. You hit the jackpot. You shouldn't spend a single second feeling anything but happy."

Brad nodded. He got what his friend was telling him, but he couldn't seem to shake the feeling that...

"You're working to hook up with her, right?" Jack asked. "You want to make her a part of all of this, don't you?"

"Yeah, I do."

"Well, if you do—"

"*If?*"

"Okay, okay." Jack waved both hands in the air. "*When*, then. When you do, she'll be riding on the happy train, too." Jack lifted his arm at a right angle and pumped his fist in the air, shouting, "Choo chooooooo!"

Brad couldn't help but laugh. Everything his friend said was true. He wanted Cathy to be a part of this. He couldn't erase all of the bad she'd suffered, but he could do everything in his power to fill her future with as much happiness as she could stand.

He waited for that feeling of relief to arrive. For the weight of that boulder sitting on his chest to dissolve.

But it didn't.

Jack gave him a backhanded slap on the shoulder. "I think you owe me a cold one for this therapy session."

"Yeah," Brad said vaguely. "You keep this up and I'll have to start calling you Dr. Jack."

Jack squared his shoulders. "I like the sound of that."

The half-cleaned display cabinet sat waiting for attention, and the order forms for the toy companies still needed filling out.

"I've got so much crap to do," he told Jack, "but..."

"I'm telling you, you just need a beer." Jack set

the screwdriver down on the cabinet top. "Tomorrow's another day."

"Okay, go get Landon," Brad suggested. "The three of us can wash up and then head over to Seacrets."

He watched Jack amble across the floor, struggling with the vague but persistent feeling of unworthiness. Jack had likened this inheritance to winning the lottery. He'd said good luck had thumped him squarely between the eyes. That he should think about this whole thing as a ride on the happy train.

Brad heaved a sigh, still uncertain he deserved a train ticket.

CHAPTER SIX

Cathy entered the Convention Center and was immediately swallowed up in a clamor of conversation, laughter, and music.

"A cacophony of sound," she murmured, grinning at her use of the Dictionary Word of the Day as she moved down the wide aisle flanked on either side with chairs toward the back of the room where a wide stage had been set up.

People were gathered in dozens of various sized clumps while others milled about the auditorium and still others waited in line at the cash bar. She said hello to those she knew, smiled at those she didn't. The attire being worn was all over the map, from the extremely casual shorts or capris and flip-flops, to jeans and t-shirts, to upscale casual trousers and tops, to the more formal suits and dresses. Cathy had taken an hour to pick out her outfit and had finally decided on a royal blue, sleeveless, v-neck wrap dress. The ruching along the side seams caused the fabric to cling to her curves. The hem struck her at mid-thigh and, along with her strappy stilettos, showed off her legs to perfection.

The idea of standing on that stage with all eyes trained on her had nerves tapping in her stomach with the ferocity of desperate dancers at an open audition of All That Jazz. She hadn't felt this freaked out in years. A vivid memory floated up through the anxiety. She'd been seven years old and had woken up in the backseat of her mom's car. The darkness had spooked her because the sky had been bright blue when her mother had told her to "lock the doors and sit tight for a few minutes," promising she'd be right back. Then Cathy had seen the eyes, wide and staring into the windows.

There must have been half a dozen noses nearly pressed to the glass. She'd screamed bloody murder for what must have been minutes but had felt like long, nightmarish hours.

Living with a drug-addicted mother had been an unpredictable and hellish existence. She silently thanked heaven for her grandmother. It mattered little that the woman had been as stern as a Marine sergeant.

But this was different, she reminded herself. Way different. She had *chosen* to be the center of attention this time. No bloody-murder screams necessary; no police officers or child protective services stepping in. This was going to be a piece of cake, and it wouldn't last for more than a few minutes. And besides that, it was all for a very good cause. The smile she forced on her lips helped her to claw her way out of the dark childhood memory. She relaxed her shoulders, took a deep, calming breath. This would be fun. She felt confident that she looked good—thank goodness for fashionable clothes that enhanced a girl's assets.

Brad stood on the stage with a few others, performing a mic check. He looked amazing in his dark, summer weight suit. The blue tie matched his eyes. It was rare that Cathy got to see him this dressed up. The magnitude of desire the sight of him stirred in her surprised her. Her steps slowed, and she took a moment to stare. But within the span of several quickened heartbeats, he looked up, and when their gazes met, she lifted her hand in greeting. He waved her up onto the stage.

When she reached the top of the stairs, he left the group and came toward her.

"You look like a million dollars," he murmured, trailing his fingers up her bare arm.

Her mouth went dry, and yearning trilled through her. "You look good yourself."

He kissed her lightly on the mouth, and she pulled away and narrowed her gaze. These public displays of affection he'd been showing recently confused her. Yes, they were intimate. Wonderfully, *deliciously* so. But they usually kept things friendly and casual when others were around.

Rather than react to her silent curiosity, he said, "They're here. Oliver and Amelia. They've brought Ethan with them."

The proceeds of tonight's fund raiser would go to the Ferguson family.

Cathy gave the crowd a quick glance, but didn't see them. "That's great."

"They're not going to stay," Brad told her. "Ethan's feeling weak today, but Oliver wanted to say a few words."

"That will be nice. But I'm glad they won't be staying." Cathy grinned. "Once these young lifeguards start strutting around this stage, the girls and guys out in the audience are going to go wild. That's not something a seven-year-old needs to witness." She looked out toward the ever growing crowd. "Did you expect this many people to show up?"

Brad's smile went wide. "No, but I'm happy to see it. I hope their pockets are full of cash. More people means more money."

"True." When she caught sight of all the lifeguards milling around behind the stage, she wrinkled her nose. "Do you really need me? I mean, look at all those fresh, young bodies... er, ah, *faces* just waiting to be auctioned off."

"Yes, I need you." He clasped her upper arms and looked into her face. "I'm not letting any of the business owners off the hook. I mean it. I'm not letting anyone chicken out."

"So I'm not the first to ask, huh?"

"No, you're not. Heather tried to get out of it."

Cathy arched her brows. "Heather's here?"

Brad nodded. "Yes. I told you she was coming. And you're both in for the duration. I need some fodder for the middle-aged crowd."

"*Hey!*" She gave his shoulder a playful shove.

He laughed. "Sorry. That's not what I meant."

She screwed up her mouth. "That's *exactly* what you meant."

He slid his arms around her and murmured, "Come on, now. Don't be upset. I'm middle-aged, myself, you know."

"And that's supposed to lift my spirits?"

His fingertips pressed into her back, urging her closer, and his voice coursed over her like warm velvet when he whispered into her ear, "Maybe I'm reminding you that time is ticking? And maybe you should think about settling down?"

Cathy let out a low, sexy chuckle. Overt flirting was usually relegated to more private surroundings, but two could play this game.

Planting her palm on his chest, she applied just enough pressure to put some space between them.

"*Nevah!*" Then she flashed him a wicked look. "But if you bid enough to win me, I just might make it worth your while later on tonight, big fella." She winked. "Now I'm going to go find Heather. I have a few choice words for that woman."

The momentum of her spin had her hair whipping into her face, but she didn't dare spoil the effect of her exit by reaching up to brush it aside. She focused all her attention on the slow sway of her hips as she walked away from him.

In their on-going game of tease and tantalize, she felt she had won this round.

She meandered among the backstage "fodder," as Brad called those who were being auctioned off, looking for Heather. The lifeguards were in high spirits. Most of them sported their daily uniform—bright red trunks for the guys and two-piece suits for the young women. They laughed and razzed each other about who would bring in the largest bid. These nubile hard-bodies would be in high demand, that's for sure. Hell, if Cathy had been fifteen years younger, she'd have been out in that audience, front row, center seat, with every nickel of her summer savings.

Chuckling, she swung her gaze to the left and caught sight of Daniel. Her steps slowed when she saw Heather standing beside him.

Good friends were like stars in the sky; you couldn't always see them, but you just knew they were there. Constant. Dependable. Oh, bright daylight or gray clouds might obscure them for a time; however, night always came, and clouds eventually passed by.

That's how Cathy felt about her friendship with Heather. It was steadfast. Permanent. The love they shared would certainly outlast this silly anger that had taken hold of Heather.

Gripping her clutch, she walked toward her friend with purpose.

Daniel saw her before Heather did.

"Cathy!" He smiled, his tone filled with pleasant surprise. "How are you? It's been ages."

He kissed her on the cheek, and Cathy returned his smile as she said, "It's been way too long, hasn't it?"

"You look great," he told her. "You're in the auction, too?"

She nodded. "Couldn't really get out of it. But it's for a great cause, so..."

"I have strict orders to bid fast and bid high." Daniel laughed.

"Heather always was the lucky one." As soon as the words left her mouth, Cathy realized her mistake. Usually she, Sara, and Heather snarked at each other constantly; taunting one another was just their way. It meant nothing, and was always followed up with a barb from the one who'd been taunted. But with the situation between her and Heather the way it was, her remark sounded nothing but rude.

Heather's eyes narrowed.

"Sorry," Cathy murmured.

The apology trailed off into awkward silence. Cathy wanted to kick herself for the bad move.

"I love your dress," she tried, but she knew the compliment was useless now. Then she said, "Brad told me Oliver and Amelia are here."

"Great." Daniel slipped his hands into his pockets. "I wonder how Ethan is doing. Do you know?"

"I don't. But he's here with his parents. Somewhere." Cathy gazed out over the crowd. "I'm sure we'll get an update on his condition at some point tonight. Brad said Oliver asked to say a few words."

Finally, Cathy could stand it no longer. The question singeing her insides burned its way to the surface. She tipped up her chin and met Heather's gaze.

"So... am I invited?"

Obvious confusion seemed to take Heather off-guard. "Invited?"

"To the *baby party*," Cathy said.

Heather's jaw dropped a fraction of an inch and her lips parted. Then she murmured, "Mia."

Cathy nodded. "She told me when she came down for pancakes. Do you need me to do anything? Help you to—"

"No."

The short, curt answer didn't deter Cathy. Softly, she said, "Sara's as big as a beach ball. You're leaving it a little late, aren't you?"

"I've been busy," Heather said. "And if I wanted your opinion, I'd have asked." Then she gave a little gasp and looked at Daniel. "Mia's with Sara now. Do you think she'll tell her about the shower?"

Daniel's brows drew together.

"Heather, don't be upset with Mia." Cathy tucked her clutch under her arm. "It's not like she meant to squeal. In fact, she didn't seem to realize that—"

"*What?*" Heather snapped out. "That she was revealing a secret?"

Cathy felt like she'd been elbowed in the diaphragm.

Anger tightened Heather's features. "Stop texting me. You're not funny. You're annoying." She touched Daniel on the arm and told him, "I'm going to the ladies room." And she walked away.

As soon as Heather was out of earshot, Cathy turned to Daniel. "When the hell is she going to forgive me?"

He looked contrite. "I keep trying. I swear. It'll happen. She just needs more time."

"But it's been a long time, Daniel."

Brad's voice blared over the speaker system with a boisterous welcome that had the crowd cheering. Then he invited the Ferguson family to the stage.

People applauded and shouted encouragement.

Cathy and Daniel moved to a spot where they could view the young couple and their son.

Oliver, a tall, gangly man, took the mic from Brad.

"Hey, ever-body," he said once the din subsided. "'Melia and I would like to take this opportunity to thank all of you for helping us. We'd like to thank the Ocean City Beach Patrol. And the Town of Ocean City. The Council Members. Me and 'Melia both know that we'd have gone bankrupt if it hadn't been for your help over the years. Ethan here—" Oliver reached out and tapped his son on the shoulder. "He woulda had to do without that special wheelchair and the walker, if it hadn't been for all the donations that we've received."

Amelia Ferguson leaned toward her husband and said, "There aren't words to express how grateful we are." Tears of gratitude welled in her big green eyes and trailed, unheeded, down her cheeks.

Seeing his mother upset, Ethan buried his face in her skirt and wrapped his arms around her knees. The mic picked up his faint words. "Don't cry, Mommy. I'm okay."

The boy was pasty and frail-looking, and he was small for his age. He'd been through hell and back; the long, lopsided scar marring his bald head proved it. The young mother smiled as she bent and clasped her child to her; her tears continued to stream and her chin quivered.

A knot rose in Cathy's throat and emotion turned her gaze fuzzy. The local residents had rallied around this little boy, this whole family, ever since he'd first been diagnosed with cancer a few years ago. At the beginning, no one expected him to live to see his next birthday, but Ethan continued to show his fighting spirit.

The boy pulled away from his mom, reached up to curl his fingers into the pocket of his dad's trousers, and he gave a yank. Oliver leaned down on one knee to hug his son.

"Can I tell 'em?" Ethan asked.

Oliver nodded and leaned the microphone toward Ethan's chin. The boy turned to face the audience.

"I *love* my wheelchair!" He shouted the words so loudly, his father flinched.

Cathy chuckled around the lump lodged around her larynx. The chattering in the audience drew her gaze, and she marveled at how many people seemed to be laughing and crying at the same time.

"I don't have to use it very often anymore,"

Ethan said. "But when I do, all I have to do is push that little lever thing and I can go fast. I can back up, too. And turn in circles."

The audience applauded, and several people in the room called out the boy's name. Ethan waved to them. When he took the mic from his dad, some people began shushing others until the room settled.

"I know Daddy has 'surance, from his job, that pays some of my doctors."

Oliver's eyes went wide at his son's words, and he started to reach for the mic.

"No, Daddy," Ethan said. "I want to talk." Then he looked out toward the audience and admitted, "I don't really know what 'surance is, exactly, but I've heard Mommy and Daddy say a gazillion times they're glad they have it."

He shifted his weight to one foot and stuffed his hand into the pocket of his shorts. Cathy grinned because he looked so comfortable addressing the crowd.

"I'm not 'posed to know about our money problems," Ethan said. "But I've overheard things. Once when I got up for a drink of water, I walked into the living room when Daddy told Mommy that, even with 'surance, we have more bills than we have money. And I know all you people are here tonight to help us, so I want to say thank you." He took his hand out of his pocket and placed it on his father's knee. "We want to say thank you, right, Dad? Very, very much."

Oliver smiled at his son and quietly prodded, "You have something else to tell them, don't you?"

"Oh yeah." Ethan grinned. "I almost forgot. I have good news. I'm in rendition!" His grin widened for an instant, but when no one reacted, he looked confused. He tried again. "Um, I'm in *rescission?*" He looked to his father for help.

"Rescission will work," Oliver said, chuckling, and he took the mic. "We *are* rescinding the power of cancer. Son, you're in remission."

"Remission!" Ethan lifted a triumphant fist into the air.

The crowd exploded, everyone jumped to their feet, clapping and whistling and chanting Ethan's name. The little boy beamed as bright as a lighthouse bulb.

Cathy clapped her hands together so hard, her palms stung.

Brad approached center stage, carrying a tall,

round package. Oliver handed over the microphone.

"Ethan, the Kite Loft donated this for you," Brad told him. "And I want to see you out on the beach flying this baby just as soon as you're feeling up to it."

The kite was twice as tall as the boy, and he grabbed it with both hands. "Whoa! Mommy, do you see this?"

"I do," she said. "It's amazing. What do you say, Ethan?"

He turned his awe-filled eyes onto Brad. "Thanks!"

"It's a phoenix," Brad told him. "Do you know what that is?"

"No. But it's big. And it's cool, too."

Brad laughed. "A phoenix is a mythological bird that... well, it keeps rising up... flying high in the sky." Addressing the crowd, he asked, "Don't you think that's a perfect symbol for Ethan?"

Again the crowd went wild. Pure elation filled Cathy to the brim. She touched her thumb and middle finger together, placed them in her mouth, and let out a loud, piercing, unladylike whistle... a talent Brad had taught her years ago during a high school football game. If Sara and Heather had been standing here with her, they might have disapproved; Cathy wouldn't have cared. She was that happy.

Oliver picked up his son, and Amelia carried the new kite. The Ferguson's waved to the crowd as they filed off stage and down the steps.

"Bye, Ethan," Brad said. "Everyone, let's give Ethan a big send off."

People shouted and continued to applaud.

Then Brad said, "Now let's get this auction started!"

CHAPTER SEVEN

The deadbolt tendered a dull thud when Cathy turned the front door key. She pushed open the door and stepped into her living room.

The house might have been tiny, but it was her treasure. The square box structure with its tall, A-frame roof contained a living room, eat-in kitchen, bathroom, and a single bedroom downstairs, and an open loft area upstairs. During her teen years, she'd slept in the loft. The slanted ceiling. No door. The hip-high railing running the full length of one side. So many times she'd lamented the lack of privacy.

But she'd never complained.

Her grandmother had taken her in, provided a safe, warm place for her to sleep every night, rescued her from the chaotic life she'd lived for the first seven years of her life with her mother.

The house was small, but it was home.

She set down her purse and keys on the side table, and inhaled sharply when she felt Brad's body press up against her back. He slid his hands around her waist and then reached up to cup her breasts.

The auction had been fun. One by one, the young men and women of the Beach Patrol team had gone out onto the stage. The twenty-somethings at the convention center had made their bids. After the first intermission, the business owners had gone up on the auction block. When it had been Cathy's turn, there had been a few bids—as promised, Al and Lyle had both lifted their paddles—and then Brad had called out an outrageous amount of money. Even now, the thought of having won the highest bid of the evening made her smile.

He touched his nose to her skin on that sensitive spot where her neck met her shoulder. She leaned her head to the side and closed her eyes, savoring the feel of his hot lips, the gentle rake of his teeth, the laving of his tongue. The light trailing of his fingers hardened her nipples into tight buds, the sensuous ministrations sending her blood thrumming through her body.

His hands settled on her hips and he nudged her to turn around. Automatically, her arms snaked around his neck, and they kissed. He tasted faintly of beer—and deep need; although the second flavor could have been entirely her imagination. She smiled against his mouth.

He urged her backward several steps, and when the sofa made contact with the back of her calves, momentum forced her to sit. She pouted when her lips, wet from his kiss, were no longer joined with his. But the sight of him removing his trousers and kicking them aside dissolved her momentary sulk.

Soft, cool fabric whooshed over her thighs as Brad loomed over her, pushing her dress higher, and higher. She let her gaze travel down the length of his torso. The hem of his dress shirt hid the most erotic bits of him, but when she looked into his face, she saw the intense desire concentrated in his deep blue eyes. She'd seen that look so many times before. She had no doubt he was granite hard. And ready.

Cathy shifted her hips, shimmied out of her panties, and then she leaned back, slid open her knees, and lifted her arms to him. He slipped into her, fully, deeply, and her breathy inhalation simmered with pure pleasure.

"When I unlocked the door," she whispered huskily in his ear, "I meant to invite you in." She couldn't stop the sumptuous grin that curled her lips. "But now there's no need, huh?"

Their hips began to move in a slow, well-orchestrated dance—one they'd performed enough times to perfect. Soon her shallow exhalations were accompanied by low, frantic moans.

She climaxed quickly; when he leaned away from her, she could tell he hadn't.

He stood, straightened his shirt, and reached for his pants.

"Whoa, whoa," she said, offering a throaty chuckle. "Hold on there, cowboy." She rose from the sofa and tugged her dress over her head and tossed it onto the couch. She stood in front of him, completely naked except for her stilettos. Smiling at him, she whispered, "It's your turn."

She reached out her hand to him, confident he would take it.

And that's exactly what he did.

As she led him through the house to her bedroom, she realized this was the reason she loved sex with Brad.

The living room, the kitchen, in the bed, on the steps, in the car, she never knew where the adventurous spirit might strike. Sometimes it was rushed, other times long and languorous. Sometimes they were tender, other times they were rough and tumble.

Right now, she intended to lie him down across her bed, straddle his gorgeous body, and take complete control. And he would let her. In fact, he would revel in the surrender. And he'd do it without feeling that his masculinity had been in any way diminished.

Of course, she'd take her shoes off first, determined to avoid poking another hole in her mattress.

Brad's confidence—in his physical appearance,

in his intelligence and talents, in his sexual prowess—appealed to her. She liked it. A lot.

"You're in trouble," she told him, the solid feel of his hand in hers reigniting her desire. "I'm about to have my way with you."

Nearly an hour later, she padded into the bathroom.

"You have to feel good about tonight," she called. "I'll bet you had to have raised close to ten thousand dollars for the Fergusons, don't you think?"

She flushed, then went to the sink to wash her hands. Over the running water, she told him, "Heather spoke to me. Just a few words. But it was better than nothing. She's still angry." Under her breath, she added, "And stubborn."

When would Heather come to understand that, although Cathy *had* betrayed her confidence, everything had turned out for the best?

"Who the hell knows?" she muttered.

Drying her hands on a towel, she wondered if Brad had fallen asleep. Then she heard the distinct sound of metal teeth as he drew his zipper closed and the jangle of his belt buckle.

She stopped in the doorway, realizing he hadn't

responded to her. In fact, she couldn't remember him having said a single word since they'd arrived at her house.

"Are you okay?"

He focused on buttoning his shirt. "It's late. I'm tired."

"Hey." She stepped into the bedroom and waited for him to look at her. "You sure you're okay?"

Brad sighed. "I'm fine."

"But I've been talking and..." She didn't bother finishing the rest of the sentence.

He snatched up his wallet and stuffed it into his back pocket. "Tonight was a great success. But I can't take the credit. Every member of the team got involved." He walked by her out into the living room, and she followed.

"Now every single one of them has to give up their next day off to fulfill all those lunch obligations."

"Speaking of obligations," she said, "when do you want me to make you lunch?"

He stared at her for a moment, and then bent to slip into his dress shoes. "I'm scheduled to work the next six days. It'll have to wait."

His tone... his whole demeanor puzzled her.

"You seem annoyed."

He picked up his suit jacket from the arm of the sofa. "Like I said. It's late. I'm tired."

"If you were too tired to come over here, why didn't you just say so?"

He moved to the front door and opened it, his mouth a flat line when he turned back to face her. "But, Cathy, this is what we do, right?"

Without another word, he stepped outside and closed the door behind him.

CHAPTER EIGHT

C athy pulled into Brad's driveway, killed the
engine, and gathered up the bags she'd packed with
food and all the necessary accoutrements for a
picnic, the items securely protected with gallon-
sized plastic zip bags. They'd decided to double up
on Brad's jet ski and ride over to their favorite out-
of-the-way sandy spot on the St. Martin's River to
eat. The heavy-duty plastic bags would protect the
food, the napkins, the plates, even her cell phone,

from the water. With a small jerk of her hip, she closed the car door, and headed toward the house.

There had been some doubt in her mind about when, or even *if*, this lunch date would take place. After Brad's odd, post-coitus demeanor at her house last weekend, she hadn't known what to think. However, he'd stopped into the café the very next morning to fill his thermos with coffee, acting as chipper as ever, so the only logical conclusion to draw regarding his behavior was that he'd been telling the truth; he'd merely been tired.

Brad came around the back corner of the house and lifted his hand in greeting. When they met, he kissed her cheek.

"Here, let me take those," he said, reaching for the bags.

"It's a pretty day." She looked toward the huge, cottony cumulus clouds hovering high in the cerulean sky.

They walked toward the shoreline.

"No rain in the forecast," he told her. "We're all gassed up and ready to go." He opened both of the jet ski's storage bins and stowed Cathy's bags. "I'm starved. I hope you brought something good to eat."

"You hope?" She pulled a face. "I'm insulted." But then she grinned. "I've made proscuitto-wrapped dates with honey balsamic syrup. And eggplant spread. And black olive and artichoke spread that I'll serve on crusty bread, and for dessert, I baked a Smith Island cake. I only brought a couple slices of that."

"Mmm, you've got me drooling." He pulled her close. "And it has little to do with food."

His husky murmur against her ear sent a delicious shiver cascading along the side of her neck and down her torso. The tickling sensation made her chuckle.

"You want to just stay here?" She teased him, but she wouldn't have minded in the least if he'd said yes.

"Let's stick to the plan." He reached into the pocket of his shorts and handed over the key. "You want to drive?"

"Absolutely."

Minutes later, the wind whipped at her hair, and sea spray showered them with each small wave she hit. Brad's smooth, warm hands were settled lightly on her waist. The speed and undulation of zipping across the bay exhilarated her and she let out a laugh.

They passed the Isle of Wight and Cathy waved at the group of teens fishing off the pier. Brad pointed toward the mouth of the St. Martin's and she slowed just a little and veered right. Less than a half mile into the wide river, she headed toward a desolate sandy beach area and slowed the jet ski until they were crawling forward.

"Hold on," she said over her shoulder.

They came to an abrupt halt when they made contact with the soft, gritty bottom. Cathy cut the engine and left the key in the ignition.

Brad hopped off the back, splashing in the few inches of water. He offered her his hand and she took it. They grabbed the bags from the bins, and then waded ashore.

"Gosh, that was so fun," she told him.

"I love being out on the water."

They immediately started clearing a small area of debris: shells, pebbles, sea grass, bottle caps, drift wood, anything that the wind and tide had washed ashore.

She dove into one of the bags. "Here's the sheet."

They worked together like a well-oiled machine; she took two corners and he took the other two, and they spread out the fabric on the sand.

"My arms are still humming." She rubbed at her upper arms. "Can we sit in the sunshine for a minute before we eat?" she asked.

"I wouldn't mind at all." He smiled as he eased down beside her.

Cathy rolled onto her back on the sheet and wriggled her bottom and then her shoulders to make an indentation in the sand. Then she reached over her head and pulled up a small mound under the fabric to use as a pillow. Molding the sand to fit the body was a normal beach-dweller action. You didn't think about it; you just did it.

Small waves lapped at the shore, nowhere near as big as over on the ocean but just as rhythmic and relaxing. The sun warmed her skin, loosened her joints, melted her bones.

"I love this place," she said. "It's so peaceful."

"Remember when we were in high school," he said, "and everyone used to meet here?"

"I do." The heat of the sun warmed her closed eyelids. "Remember the time we started that bonfire?"

"You mean the fire we started without a permit? And the Coast Guard showed up less than an hour after the first sparks were struck?"

"Yup. That's the one. We never did find out who reported us, did we?"

"Nope." He tapped the side of her knee with the back of his hand. "It was a hell of a coincidence that Jerri was with us that night, *and* that her brother was in the Coast Guard, *and* that Jerri's brother was on that boat."

"Coincidence? It was a freakin' miracle." The memory made Cathy grin.

"If it hadn't been for Jerri's brother," Brad said, "we'd have all ended up at the county courthouse in Snowhill in front of the juvie judge."

"Grandmom would have had a conniption fit." She chuckled. "I remember you were with a different girl almost every weekend."

"Oh, come on, now. I wasn't that bad."

She felt him shift on the sand beside her.

"Weren't you?"

Her belly clenched when she laughed. "You were a horny toad. You treated us girls like we were a big box of salt water taffy, and you were determined to taste each one."

"Horny toad," he muttered under his breath. "I was bad, huh? Am I ever going to live down that reputation?"

"Why would you want to?" Without thinking, she reached out her hand a few inches and dug her fingers into the sand. "You were a good looking guy. And all the girls liked you. They clamored after you, if I recall. Even me." Her tone sobered as she added, "None of us skipped our turn. And some of us were lucky enough to have more than one go round."

When he didn't respond, she peeked at him through her lashes and saw that he was staring off across the water.

"Hey, the reputation thing is really bothering you." After making the observation, she lifted her head and shielded her eyes from the sun's glare. His continued silence urged to her sit up. "Brad?"

"Yeah," he told her softly. "It's bothering me."

"What are you talking about? You've reveled in being a ladies man. What's going on?" She leaned forward so she could see his face better. "Is one of your lady friends putting on the pressure? Somebody wanting you to settle down? You *have* been acting a little weird lately."

He swiveled his head, his gaze zeroing in on hers. "I don't have any lady friends, Cathy."

She barked out a laugh. "Right! Listen to me, you have more babes than there are crabs in Assawoman Bay." As soon as the words left her mouth, she sniggered. "That probably wasn't the best metaphor to use when referring to your sex life."

Sudden annoyance sparked in his blue eyes, and her humor waned.

"Just because you see me in a nightclub with a woman," he told her, his voice going tight, "doesn't mean I'm sleeping with her."

"Okay," she answered, lifting her palms in surrender. The last thing she wanted to do was get into an argument.

After a moment, she softly asked, "What's going on, Brad?"

"I know you think our relationship is unconventional. I know you like the game you think we're playing." He paused long enough to moisten his lips. "It excites you. You find it titillating."

"I find it *titillating*?" One corner of her mouth

pulled back. "Did you just fall out of a Regency romance novel or something?"

The things he said... the things he *insinuated* bemused her, and she could easily see the whole day going to hell in a handcart. Cracking a joke had been her way of attempting to ease the tension.

He shifted on the sand so that he was facing her. "Let me ask you something. Why do you enjoy the whole sleeping around thing, Cathy?"

"*I* don't sleep around."

"I thought as much."

"I sleep with *you*."

"Yeah, you do."

"*You're* the one who sleeps around."

It was as if they'd fallen into some sort of fast and furious video game where they zinged each other with laser guns.

"If that's what you think is happening," he said, "then that makes me... not a very nice person, right? Maybe you should ask yourself why you find it so exciting to be used by me."

Her lips parted but no sound came out. She felt as if he'd snatched the breath right out of her throat.

She dragged in a lungful of air, and then words started spewing.

"I'm not *titillated* by the idea of being used." Her emphasis made the word sound ugly. "I don't think about our relationship that way."

Unable to remain still, she shot to her feet. "What we have between us—" she pointed from herself to him and back again several times as if her wrist were loosely hinged "—offers me *freedom*. *Sweet* freedom. I'm free to see you *when* I want, and *if* I want. I'm free to have sex with you when I want and if I want. I can—"

"There it is!" He launched off the sheet. "*There's* the difference."

Cathy snapped her jaw closed, wondering what the hell he was talking about.

"You have sex with me," he ground out. "I make love to you."

"You have lost your mind," she said. And then she turned and began stalking down the beach. If she didn't get away from him, she just might give him a good slug.

"You'd better check your Dictionary of the Day. They're not the same thing," he bellowed after her.

"And don't walk away from me when I'm talking to you!"

Stark white fury blinded her. No man ordered her around anymore. Not since she'd shaken herself free of her ex. Todd had spent years dictating how she would live; what she could say, where she could work, how and when she could spend money, whom she could call a friend. That sort of treatment wouldn't start again. No way. No how. She spun around and raced toward him, and she didn't stop until they were nearly nose to nose.

"It's Word of the Day, Pal," she spit out. "It's about *words*. Not concepts. *And don't you dare tell me what to do.*"

"You are the most infuriating woman I have ever met."

They glared at each other.

"For weeks," he said, "I've been trying to show you... to tell you that our relationship *isn't* what you think. I am *not* what you think. This isn't some kind of game I'm playing with you, Cathy."

Her brow furrowed. "Of course, it's a game. It's always been a game. And most of the time it's fun. But some of the time, Brad—like this very moment—it's a pain in the ass."

He shook his head, his eyes never wavering from hers. "What are we doing? Where is this road we're on taking us? 'Cause I don't mind admitting that I feel lost."

Ire got the better of her. "Why does it have to take us anywhere?" she yelled.

The shout was a great release of pent-up frustration, and besides, no one was around for miles.

"Because I'm done with games. I want more. I *need* more, Cathy."

She let out a bark of laughter, sharp and harsh. "Of what? This? Harping at each other? Arguing? If that's so, you really are nuts."

"Don't do that," he said. "Don't demean what we have. What we are. We're good together, and you know it. I want to be in a committed relationship with you. I want you to marry me, damn it!"

Until this moment, she hadn't even been certain what they'd been arguing about. She and Brad had always walked a fine line between romantic, sexy intimacy and easy, breezy friendship. It worked for them. It had worked for them just fine for years now. But now he was bringing up the dreaded "m" word. What the hell was going on? She felt as if the world suddenly spun out of control; as if she lived in one of those cheap, seaside snow globes found in every souvenir shop in town and someone had picked it up and given it a good, hard shake.

"*Marry you?*" she said, every ounce of her incredulity evident in the short question. "I'm not going to marry you. I'm not going to marry anyone. Ever again."

"I'm nothing like that asshole you divorced."

His tone was low and ominous, and for some reason, it stoked the fires of Cathy's anger.

"You're damned straight about that! If you were, I'd have nothing to do with you." The words burst from her like pebbles from a slingshot. Then an odd thought struck her like one of her ex's unexpected cuffs to the jaw. She tilted her head and asked, "Did you just propose to me in the middle of an argument?"

The idea was hysterical; funny as hell, really. She should be holding her stomach, rolling on the sand with laughter. So why did she continue to seethe inside?

Apparently, Brad failed to see the humor in the question, too. Fury darkened his expression.

"Yeah," he said, his chin lifting unapologetically.

"Yeah, I did. And it's because the only time we ever fight is when I have an idea, or an opinion, or a want or need that differs from yours."

"What the hell are you talking about? You're free to have all the ideas and opinions you want."

"Am I? Am I, really? Why do you think I didn't tell you about the arcade, Cathy?"

The muscles of his face were taut.

"Could it be because I knew you'd tell me all the reasons why the business wouldn't be a success? Maybe you ought to ask yourself why you *always* find it necessary to—"

"Well, I'll be damned," she whispered. "So *that's* what this is about. Now I get it. You want me to marry you so I'll help you pay off the mortgage on that stupid mini-golf course."

His face flamed with fury. "I don't owe a mortgage, Cathy!"

He could have been speaking in some foreign language for all she knew. What was important was what she saw; in the periphery of her vision, she deciphered the raising of his hand, and in an instant, she was catapulted back in time.

CHAPTER NINE

Instinct alone had her flinching into a protective stance—she turned her face to the side, her hands raised, the shoulder closest to him lifted to absorb the anticipated blow, her eyelids clenched shut, and her neck muscles tensed so tightly a spasm of pain arrowed up into her skull.

When she opened her eyes, she was staring down at the sand beneath her feet, still on her feet. No punch had been thrown. No pain rolled over her body.

A gull cried overhead.

She let out her breath slowly, relaxed her shoulders, and lifted her gaze to Brad's.

Intense perplexity wrinkled his forehead as he stared at her.

A fiery heat burst to life in Cathy's chest and rose to singe her neck and face, scorch her scalp. The utter mortification forced her to avert her gaze, burned the sockets of her eyes with unshed tears.

A sudden, all-encompassing frailty permeated her being, chinking her armor. She felt weak. Vulnerable.

And completely humiliated.

The sole thought running through her head was to get away from the helplessness. Escape the situation.

"I'm leaving," she announced, and she raced toward the jet ski as if her life depended on it. And in her mind, her life as she knew it was in jeopardy. The strong, independent woman she'd worked so hard to create had been suddenly invaded by the broken and abused person she had once been.

"Cathy!" Brad called after her, his tone unyielding. "Don't you even think about leaving me here."

She was up to her ankles, pushing the jet ski into deeper water when she screamed, "You can't tell me what to do!"

Straddling the jet ski, she reached to turn the key when he shouted her name again. Tears streamed down her cheeks as she turned her gaze toward shore.

She knew the man standing on the sand was not Todd Kirkland, knew she was safe from physical harm, but reason wasn't enough to thaw the icy fear and shame that clawed through her veins and urged her to flee. She turned the key, heard the machine rumble to life. Cathy cranked the throttle and the engine roared.

Again, she looked back.

That's Brad. That's Brad. That's Brad.

Her brain shouted the silent chant, over and over.

Glowering at him, she finally lifted her hand and motioned for him.

Brad reached down, snatched up the corners of plastic sheet, and gathered the bags holding their lunch, like a big hobo-bag. He splashed to the jet ski and opened the storage bin.

"If you're coming," she said over her shoulder, "get on. Now."

The instant she sensed the weight of him behind her, she engaged the clutch and took off across the water. He grabbed onto her to keep from being flung off the back.

"Slow down," he warned.

The sun beat down on her head. The water tasted salty on her lips. The warmth of his hands penetrated the cotton of her t-shirt. Even these normal, everyday sensations weren't enough to calm the terror that had thrown her world off-kilter.

"The water's too shallow for this speed," he yelled, the wind whipping at the words.

Whatever made contact with the bottom of the jet ski—a crab trap, a rock, a tree stump—she would never know. The grating sound filled the air, deafening her. And then they were airborne.

She hit the water with a splash, her bottom and back striking the sandy bottom with enough force to rattle her teeth. Stars danced in her hazy vision and briny water and sand flooded her mouth and eyes. She coughed and shoved herself to her feet in the thigh-deep water.

What she noticed first was the quiet. She swiped the water and grit from her eyes, coughed and spat.

"Brad!"

She saw the jet ski, its engine silenced as it bobbed upside down a few yards away. Plastic zip bags floated on the surface of the river. She identified the many-layered cake and the sliced baguette she'd so painstakingly prepared for lunch.

"Brad!" Panic constricted her throat to the point that her voice was barely recognizable. She scanned the area frantically, and the instant she found him, she slogged through the muddy water as fast as she could.

He lay on his side, deathly still, atop a tangle of exposed roots and reeds. Blood trickled from a cut high on his forehead. His eyes were closed, his ear, jaw, and neck submerged. She couldn't tell if he was dead or alive.

Her forward momentum pushed a small wall of water at him. The waves hit his stomach and quickly rolled along his chest, over his chin, and across his mouth and nose. She expected him to rise, to sputter, to cough, but he didn't move. Alarm gripped her like a tight fist.

"Brad?" She spoke softly, more for her own comfort than anything else.

She leaned over him until her ear nearly touched his nose. He was breathing, thank God. She smacked his cheek lightly, calling his name again.

She'd thought she knew a little something about first aid. She'd taken a CPR course, and she knew how to perform the Heimlich maneuver for choking victims, although she'd only had to use it once in all the years she'd run the café. She knew how to care for cuts and burns that happened while working in a professional kitchen. But she knew nothing about head injuries, or spinal injuries. Had no idea how bad off Brad might be.

"I'm sorry. I'm so very sorry."

As she murmured the words she knew he couldn't hear, she pulled off her t-shirt, rolled it into a loose, soggy ball, and gently nudged it under the side of his head to keep his face above water. Plain old common sense urged her to move him as little as possible. His back might have been broken in the accident, or his neck.

Dear God help her; he could be bleeding inside for all she knew.

Panic waged a battle with her momentary, oh-sotenuous hold on reason. She looked around her. Thick reeds and spiny-leafed vegetation covered the nearby riverbank, rendering it nearly impossible to traverse for very far let alone the distance it would take to reach a road or house. The Route 90 bridge spanned the river in the distance, ant-sized cars traveling across its expanse mere yards above the waterway. Several fishing boats looked to be anchored near the cement bridge supports. Far out into the bay, another boat dragged a skier in its wake. Cathy shouted and waved her arms, but she quickly realized everyone she could see was too far away to hear her.

On the far side of the bay, the Ocean City skyline sat against a blue sky background.

Never had she felt so desperate, or so alone.

She could make her way back to the sandy beach and hope that a boater or others on jet skis might happen by, but leaving Brad seemed out of the question. The rising tide posed an ominous threat for someone who was unconscious, and she didn't dare try to move him.

Then she remembered her phone. Brad had stowed it in one of the jet ski's rear storage bins. Cathy waded through the water toward the overturned water craft; she had to weave through rotting tree stumps.

How could she have been so stupid to fly through the water on the jet ski so close to shore?

She felt around under the water and quickly discerned that both bin doors were open. Plastic bags littered the area, the air trapped inside each allowing them to float on the surface. One by one, she picked them up, swiftly examined them, and then tossed them closer toward the shoreline. The zip lock of the bag holding the stuffed dates had been torn open, leaving the proscuitto a waterlogged mess. She tossed the bag with the others. All the while, she kept turning to check on Brad who remained motionless.

The current had carried a couple of bags further out into the mouth of the bay. Now chest deep in the water, Cathy was about to swim out to retrieve them when she heard the familiar yet muffled ringtone of her phone. The sound seemed to be coming from somewhere close to Brad. Using wide, powerful arm strokes, she propelled herself in that direction.

She snatched up a bag that was hovering just below the water's surface. The plastic was torn and full of water. The delicate pastry crust she'd wrapped around the wedge of brie earlier this morning had nearly disintegrated.

The ring sounded again, causing Cathy to drop the cheese and rush toward the water's edge. Black-shelled mussels clung to the rugged shoreline. She ripped open the bag and saw Heather's name lit up in the phone's window. Cathy slid her finger across the screen to answer.

"Heather!" Her voice was shaking. "I've wrecked the jet ski. I need you to—"

"Don't say another word," her friend cut her off sharply. "This isn't a damned game, Cathy. Sara's water broke. If she doesn't go into labor, they're going to induce."

"But—"

"She's asking for you."

A trickle ran down Cathy's arm, the warmth of it tickling her skin. She unwittingly swiped at the area and was shocked to see her hand covered in crimson. She took the phone in her blood-slippery fingers and looked at the underside of her arm. There, just above her elbow, she saw a gash deep enough to expose the stringy muscle tissue. Her stomach went queasy.

"Oh, dear Lord," she breathed into the phone. "There's blood. I'm hurt."

"Damn it, Cathy!" Heather shouted. "Stop crying wolf. Get your ass to the hospital. Sara needs—"

The phone went dead. Cathy pulled it from her ear and looked at the blank, black screen. She pressed the home button, but the screen remained black. And that's when she noticed the water slowly dripping from the bottom of the phone's case.

CHAPTER TEN

The sturdy, stern-faced ER nurse who stood between Cathy and the hallway leading to the other exam rooms looked to be in her mid-fifties; the last name printed on her ID badge was a jumble of consonants that rendered it practically unpronounceable. The woman had been smiling just ten seconds before, but the instant Cathy had slipped off the table and inched toward the door, Nurse Nan stepped into her path.

The nurse's arms were now crossed over her ample chest and she frowned.

"I told you to sit tight," she said. "That arm of yours is going to need stitches. If you bump it on anything... even if you don't bump it, that wound could start bleeding again. Get back up on that table. The doctor will be in to take care of you in just a few minutes."

"But I'd like to check on—"

"Your husband is in good hands."

"He's not my husband."

"He's where he needs to be." The woman stood her ground. "And you're where you need to be."

Finally, Cathy gritted her teeth and climbed back onto the examination table.

She hadn't believed her luck when the fishing boat had chugged its way around the marshy outcropping where she had wrecked the jet ski. The man had been so focused on following the buoyed crab line, that he hadn't seen her for the longest time. The boat's engine had drowned out her calls for help. So she'd begun throwing the plastic bags of food, in the hopes of getting his attention. It had taken not one but two well-aimed hits to the hull to make the old guy look up.

Thankfully, he'd had a radio onboard, and the Coast Guard had reached them in less than fifteen minutes. The fisherman had stayed with Cathy and Brad until the rescuers arrived.

They had fitted Brad with a neck brace before securing him to a backboard. An ambulance had met them at the nearest boat dock, and with lights and sirens blaring, the EMTs had whisked them to Atlantic General.

"Let me take a look at your arm." Nurse Nan began to unwrap the pressure bandage that one of the EMTs had applied. "I'll clean it up, and you'll be ready when the doctor comes in." Blood stained the length of gauze she pulled away from Cathy's arm. "Well, now this isn't too bad. But the ambulance tech was right. You're going to need a few stitches. What did you cut your arm on?"

"I have no idea," Cathy said. Her gaze kept darting toward the door. She wished she knew how Brad was doing. He never stirred during the boat ride or the drive in the ambulance. When they'd arrived at the hospital, the ER staff wouldn't allow her to go back with him.

"I didn't even know I was hurt," she told the woman, "until I felt the blood dripping down my arm." She frowned at the nurse. "Look, would you mind going back there to see how he's doing? This cut won't get any worse in the three minutes it will take for you to pop back there for a quick check. I'd feel a whole lot better if I knew he was awake. And if he's still not awake, I really need to know what's wrong with him. Why is he still unconscious?"

"Listen, I want you to calm down." The nurse dabbed the wound with a sterile pad moistened with disinfectant.

The sting made Cathy jerk and suck in a sharp breath.

"Sorry," Nurse Nan murmured. "The pain won't last long." She fanned at the wound and frowned. "I see sand in there. This is going to take a little longer than I first thought. As soon as I get you cleaned up, I'll go check on him. But I can only give you information if you're family."

"Oh, well, I'm his—"

Wife, she'd been about to brazenly lie through her teeth when Nurse Nan shot her an arched brow look that reminded Cathy of her earlier admission.

"The privacy laws are nothing to mess around with," she said. "You could get me into some serious trouble."

Averting her gaze, Cathy admitted, "I'm just worried. He wouldn't wake up." Softly, she added, "He must be hurt really bad."

A rush of unexpected emotion welled inside her with the strength of a tsunami. The guilt and anguish and regret rolled over her like a wall of water, threatening to drown her. Her throat swelled and tears burned her eyes like acid.

"This is all my fault." Wrenching out those mousy, thin-sounding syllables from around the jagged-edged rock of remorse lodged in her throat caused her physical pain. "I was driving the jet ski. He told me to slow down. I didn't listen."

She began to tremble and her shoulders shook with her sobs. "What if he has brain damage from hitting his head? *Oh, dear God.* What if he's paralyzed? What if he doesn't wake up? What if he dies?"

Hot tears ran, unchecked, down her face, splashing onto her t-shirt that was stiff from the briny river water. Guilt writhed in her gut.

The nurse patted her shoulder. "Honey, you need to stop this. You know very little about your friend's condition. Yes, he was unconscious when he arrived. But that could change at any moment.

You need to think good thoughts." She started bustling around the exam room. "First things first. You get that cut stitched up. Then we need to contact your friend's next of kin."

The phrase made Cathy's eye go round.

"Don't go off the deep end on me, now," Nan said softly. "Don't read anything into that. We need to contact them, is all I meant. To let them know what's going on. Maybe they can come be with you."

"Brad's parents live in Florida."

"Well, if they say it's okay, I'll mark down in his file that you can receive updates on his condition." The woman set a packet containing a sterile needle and another of suture thread on a stainless steel table. "But I need their permission first."

Relief made Cathy light-headed and she nodded, but her wretchedness didn't abate. Brad had been hurt because of her stupidity, and that wasn't something she could ever change.

There was a light knock at the door and a white-coated Asian woman pushed open the door. She couldn't have been five feet tall, and it was impossible for Cathy to guess her age.

"Someone in here need to be stitched up?"

Cathy swiped at her eyes with the back of her free hand. "That would be me."

"Nancy," the doctor said, "are you making the patients cry again?"

The question was meant for levity, Cathy was certain, and she tried to smile. She really tried.

Nurse Nan turned from the cabinet, a syringe in one hand and a small glass bottle of anesthetic in the other. "This is Doctor Lee," she told Cathy. "As you just witnessed, her comedic talent is sorely lacking. But lucky for you, she has the best suturing skills in the hospital. I wouldn't be surprised if you end up with a scar that's barely visible."

The nurse and the doctor paused for her reaction, so she tipped up her chin and said, "Yippee."

Over two hours and seven stitches later, Cathy stepped into the elevator and punched the button that would take her to the maternity ward. Exhaustion weighed on her like a strong pull of gravity.

Calling Brad's parents had been one of the most difficult things she'd ever had to do. Nurse Nan had logged onto the internet and helped Cathy find the correct phone number. Although she'd promised herself she'd hold it together, Cathy had cried as she explained to Mrs. Henderson about the accident. The woman had kindly repeated several times, "It was an accident," but that hadn't alleviated the anguish that sat like a brick in Cathy's stomach.

Brad's mother planned to book the next flight north for herself and her husband, and Cathy promised the woman she'd stay at the hospital until they arrived. That had been when Nurse Nan had taken the phone and Cathy had stepped a few feet way; however, she'd overheard that Brad was still unconscious, his vital signs were steady, and he was awaiting x-rays and an MRI.

After disconnecting the call, Nan had told Cathy that Mrs. Henderson gave her permission for the staff to talk to Cathy about Brad's condition. The woman, knowing Cathy was without a working cell phone, also promised to page Cathy if either of the Hendersons called for her or if Brad's condition changed. The nurse's kindness had Cathy's chin quivering and fresh tears flowing.

"I'm not usually this emotional," Cathy had told her.

The elevator doors opened and Heather stood directly in front of her.

Their gazes met, and Heather looked momentarily surprised, then she scowled.

"Where have you..."

The reprimand petered out as Heather took in Cathy's state. The instant she noticed the bandage on Cathy's forearm, every nuance of annoyance dissolved.

"What happened?" Heather asked.

The two of them had been standing there long enough that the elevator doors began to slide shut; Heather stuck out her arm to trigger the sensor that had the doors springing wide open again. She reached in and took Cathy by the uninjured arm and gently pulled her into the hallway.

Cathy felt as if she were about to fall apart, and the unexpected compassion on Heather's face, in her gentle touch, was her complete undoing. Tears welled in Cathy's eyes, splintering her vision into dozens of shards of bright light. Her knees went so wobbly, she feared they wouldn't hold her weight.

"Brad and I got into a fight. I wrecked the jet ski.

Brad hit his head. He was unconscious. He's still unconscious." She pressed her hand to her mouth, trying to hold in the fear that threatened to consume her.

"Oh, honey," Heather crooned. "Come sit down." She led her to a small alcove off the hallway. "Sit. Sit. Honey, I'm so sorry. I thought you were joking around on the phone earlier. I'm sorry."

Cathy shook her head, tears trailing down her face. "It's okay. How could you know? I've been sending you asinine texts. What else could you think but that I was continuing to be an ass?"

Heather scooted closer to the edge of the seat. "Tell me what happened. Tell me about the argument, I mean."

The story gushed from her like some tragic crude oil spill along the coastline, seeping into vulnerable and fragile places. When she finished, Cathy felt spent, wanting only to curl up in a ball someplace quiet.

"Wait," Heather said softly. "He asked you to marry him? And that made you angry?"

"It wasn't the proposal. It was more that—" Cathy frowned. "Maybe it *was* that he asked, or maybe *how* he asked. I don't know. After what I went through with Todd, I never want to... Marriage isn't something I want to go through again." When she unwittingly leaned her bandaged arm on the chair, she winced. "And besides that, Brad was ordering me around. Demanding things. He sounded just like Todd." Fresh tears sprang to her eyes, but she dashed at them with her crooked index finger. Faintly, she added, "He's never done that before. He's always been so easy-going. So... accommodating. To me. To my needs, my wants, my wishes. It was confusing. It was scary."

Heather gently asked, "You really thought he was going to hit you?"

"I didn't. Honestly." Cathy believed that with all her heart. She and Brad could argue with the best of them, but he'd never revealed an ounce of the kind of harmful intent she'd suffered at the hands of her ex. When she and Brad disagreed, their usual course of action was avoidance. They'd just go their separate ways for a few days, or a week, or however long it took for the argument to blow over. It was a method that worked for them.

"His commands annoyed me." Her bark of

laughter contained no humor. "Hell, I was furious. And baffled, to tell you the truth. I got all tangled up in the past... because it *felt* like the past, if that makes any sense. It was just..." Although she looked Heather in the face, she was standing back on that sandy shore. "He was angry. Demanding. I saw his hand lift. And I ducked."

"Oh, honey." Heather reached out and touched her knee.

"Brad looked stunned. And then—" Cathy's whole body tensed with the shame of it. "He knew, Heather. He *knew*." She bit her bottom lip. "I've never in my life felt so humiliated."

"But you shouldn't. It wasn't your fault that—"

"*It was*," Cathy insisted. "I let it happen, Heather. I stayed too long. I took it. I allowed it. I made excuses for it." Gazing down the hallway with unseeing eyes, she realized that she needed to put a name to *it*. She murmured, "I made excuses for the abuse. For far too long."

"Okay, so," Heather said, evidently intent on drawing Cathy back from the past, "he knows? Brad knows what you went through? You talked about it?"

The sigh Cathy released conveyed her

weariness. "Oh, hell no. I couldn't do that. I just... couldn't. I was too embarrassed to tell him."

An awful revelation hit her. "And now I might never get the chance."

Heather took her hand. "Honey, everything will be okay. You'll see. Brad is strong. He's healthy. He's going to come out of this just fine."

Oh, how she'd missed Heather. How she'd missed this sister-like sustenance. Friends were your chosen family. They were there for you because they wanted to be. They supported you out of love, not out of some sense of obligation.

What the hell was the matter with her that she'd jeopardized her friendship with Heather the way she had?

"I'm so sorry, Heather." Sliding closer, Cathy clasped Heather's hand in both of hers and held on tightly. "I'm so sorry that I hurt you. I'm sorry that I betrayed you like I did."

She paused long enough to swallow. The concern that had softened Heather's face just an instant before turned melancholic.

"I get it now," Cathy said. "I want you to know that. I fully understand exactly what I did. I made you feel vulnerable. I peeled back your protective blanket. I exposed all the bad things you felt about... yourself. And I am so sorry. I truly am." She licked her lips. "It would be like... if you had told Brad about my bruises, my black eyes, my broken nose."

"I would never have done that," Heather whispered.

"I know. And I never should have told Daniel your secret." Cathy gazed at her friend with intense love, hoping to convey all she was feeling. "Instead of being flip, instead of sending you stupid texts in the hopes that you'd get over it, I should have apologized. Over and over. I should have kept apologizing until you understood just how sorry I am." She squeezed Heather's hand. "Because I am."

Heather's eyes filled with tears; Cathy cried, too.

"You mean the world to me," Cathy said.

They hugged each other tightly, and for just a moment, the burden sitting heavily on Cathy's shoulders lifted just a little.

When they parted, Cathy said, "Tell me what's going on with Sara. Is she okay? Did she have the baby?"

"Not yet," Heather told her. "But she's in labor.

She had a couple of heavy contractions this morning. She's been under so much stress."

Cathy nodded. "I know. Landon has been dragging his heels about the wedding. Geneva's been pushy about the plans."

Now Heather nodded. "I *know*. It's been awful."

"Maybe between the two of us, we can figure out how to help her deal with it better."

"I think Mother Nature's figuring it out for her." Heather tucked a wayward strand of dark hair behind her ear. "The doctor said stress can cause early contractions. He wasn't happy with Landon, let me tell you."

"I hope the doctor gave him hell," Cathy said. "Geneva needs a talking to, as well."

"After the contractions, Sara's water broke. The doctor told her to meet him here. I think he was going to decide whether or not to induce labor, but he didn't have to. Sara's contractions continued and they're pretty regular now."

"Is the baby okay, though? She's early."

Heather's eyes went round. "I think so. Sara's hooked up to 2 different monitors and a couple of IVs. There's more beeping in there than a Friday night traffic jam. Girl, you've got to go in there and see the equipment."

"I look a mess." Cathy smoothed her palm over her hair. "I can't let her see me like this."

"You look like you've been in a jet ski accident," Heather teased. "Come on. What's a little briny stink among friends?"

They stood up.

"Okay, but I can't stay long. I should go down and check on Brad. They might know something more by now. His parents are going to want to know what's happening."

"We'll just say hi," Heather said. "Sara won't be in the mood for more than that. And then I'll pop over to your house and bring you some fresh clothes."

"That sounds heavenly."

Clasped arm in arm, they walked toward the maternity ward.

CHAPTER ELEVEN

He looked like he was sleeping. Having been cleaned up, the wound on his head didn't look bad at all. The cut hadn't required sutures, and only a small lump and slight bruising showed beneath the single, small steri-strip.

Cathy sat by Brad's bed, keeping vigil, just as she'd promised his mother she would do. Even if she hadn't made the promise, she wouldn't be anywhere else but right here. She was the reason Brad was in that bed; she couldn't rest until she saw with her own eyes that he was okay. And if he wasn't okay when he woke up...

Icy fear seeped through to the marrow. Well, she would never forgive herself.

His hand lay on the outside of the sheet, an oxygen monitor clipped to his middle finger. At least a dozen times she had reached out to take his hand in hers, but each and every time she'd drawn back before making contact. She desperately wanted to feel the warmth of him, assure herself that he really was alive, but she didn't deserve to touch him. Not after what she'd done.

The light tap on the door drew her attention, and seeing Landon there, Cathy made to stand. But he lifted both hands and motioned for her to remain seated.

"Is Sara okay?" she asked him. "Has the baby arrived?"

"No baby yet." He kept his voice quiet. "Sara's tired. Things progress a bit, and then they slack off. She's dilated five centimeters, though, so that's good. The doctor said it could be a few more hours." He took a half step further into the room. "Listen, Jack called me earlier. He was supposed to meet Brad at the arcade at four today, and when Brad didn't show up..."

"Oh." Cathy shook her head. "I didn't think to call Jack."

"He called me an hour or so ago," Landon said. "He's here. Is it okay if—"

"Sure, sure." Cathy stood up.

Landon turned, glanced out into the hallway, and beckoned.

Jack entered and nodded a greeting at her.

"I'm sorry I didn't call you, Jack," Cathy said. "I didn't think..."

"It's okay. Do his parents know what's going on?"

"Yes, I talked to his mom myself." Cathy placed her palms together, laced her fingers. "They're on their way. His parents, I mean. I was able to give them an update before they left."

"That's good," Landon said.

Jack nodded as he gazed over at Brad. "Can you tell us how he's doing?"

Cathy couldn't imagine Brad not wanting his friends to know about his condition. "He has what's called an arterio, um, something malformation. An AVM." She closed her eyes and tried again. "An arteriovenous malformation. That's it. It's a tangle of veins in his brain. It was something he was born with, I think. And when he hit his head, it began to bleed."

"Bleeding on the brain?" Concern pulled at the corners of Jack's mouth.

"The bleeding has stopped," Cathy rushed to assure him. "That's what I was told. His vital signs are stable, and he's scheduled for a follow-up MRI in the morning."

She looked from Jack to Landon. "They're treating this conservatively and they keep telling me they expect him to wake up soon."

The ICU nurse appeared in the doorway. "I'm sorry," she said softly, "but someone's got to go. Two visitors in the room only."

"I'll go," Landon said to the nurse. He looked at Cathy. "I'm sure Sara's wondering where I am. Call me if anything changes, okay?"

"I will," she promised.

Once Jack and Cathy were alone, he asked, "What happened?"

"I wrecked the jet ski." She swallowed; her voice sounded like rusty hinges. "It was my fault, Jack. It was completely my fault."

She thought she might cry, but her eyes remained remarkably dry. It seemed there were no more tears in her.

Jack sighed and stuffed his hands into the pockets of his trousers. "He's a good guy." He stared at Brad for several long moments and then glanced at Cathy. "He's a really good guy, Cathy."

The simple statement sounded like an admonishment.

"I know that."

"Do you?"

The calmly spoken question belied the emotion tensing Jack's facial muscles. A frown bit into Cathy's brow and she remained silent.

"Would it have been so difficult for you to be happy for him about the arcade?" Without waiting for her answer, he looked over toward the hospital bed as he added, "Brad had such high hopes that the new business would—" his tone quieted to a whisper "—change things."

Jack pulled his hands free from his pockets so quickly that Cathy heard the jingle of coins or keys.

"I'm going to go," he told her.

"Wait." Cathy touched his arm. "Brad said

something today I didn't understand. He said he didn't owe a mortgage on the arcade. How can that be?"

He shook his head. "You'll have to talk to Brad about that."

"Well, what did you mean?" she pressed. "When you said he thought the arcade would change things? I don't understand."

He pressed his lips together. Finally, he sighed. "I didn't mean anything. I should have kept my mouth shut. It's none of my business. I'm going to go." He pulled a business card out of his pocket. "Would you call me if his condition changes?"

Her frown only deepened as she accepted the card. "Sure."

"Day or night," he told her. "Doesn't matter. Just call." He turned toward the door and then turned back, concern etched in the lines of his face. "You should treat him nicer, Cathy. Stop being such a downer. Stop making light of his job. Why are you always so critical? He works hard. He saves lives, for crying out loud. He deserves respect for what he does. For *who* he is. He's a good man. You'll never find one who's better. You can take that to the bank."

Jack held her gaze, and then he left the room.

Hours later, when the hallways were empty and quiet, Cathy's mind still churned over Jack's comments.

Brad had such high hopes that the new business would change things.

He's a really good guy.

He deserves respect.

He works hard.

Would it have been so difficult for you to be happy for him?

Stop being a downer.

He's a good man.

Jack hadn't spoken in anger, and it sure sounded like he was making a plea on Brad's behalf. But the man's disapproval couldn't have been made clearer. The strange thing was, she hadn't felt offended. She completely agreed with many of the things Jack had said.

Brad *was* a good guy. No one could dispute that. He *was* dedicated to his job as a lifeguard. He loved it, in fact; and he *did* work hard.

As to Jack's other claims—about her being "a downer," about her not treating Brad right, about her making light of his job, being critical, not respecting him—Cathy felt slightly baffled.

She *had* questioned Brad about his new arcade venture, but she viewed that as being practical, one concerned, business-minded friend to another. She'd want him to do the same for her if she were to ponder a career change. And she teased him often about working in a profession where nearly all his colleagues were in their late teens and early twenties. She'd even called him Peter Pan in the past... the boy who refused to grow up. She'd never meant any disrespect. It was all in fun. Just playful vexing. He did the same to her. Or, at least, he *used* to, and it had driven her half nuts because... well, because...

Because she'd liked him so much back then. And she'd wanted him to feel the same way about her.

She stared out the window, studied the gibbous moon, as a memory swarmed her mind like a hive of bees.

Nineteen and all on her own on a Saturday night. Cathy drove the full length of Ocean City, looking for someone to hang out with. Neither Heather nor Sara were in town, and she couldn't believe there was no one around she knew. She couldn't stay out long because she had to work the next day, but she was antsy over the great opportunity that had come her way.

At the restaurant where she was waiting tables for the summer, there had been a huge blow up and the owner had fired one of the line cooks. Cathy wasn't sure exactly how it had happened, but while she was in the kitchen to drop off an order she'd noticed a strip steak sizzling in a pan to the smoking point. She hadn't even thought about it; she'd simply rounded the island that separated the cooks from the wait staff, she'd grabbed a pair of tongs and turned the steak over. That's all she'd done, and the next thing she knew, the head chef, James, was shouting instructions at her so she could complete the meal. Once she'd slipped the steak into the oven to finish cooking, she'd sautéed the haricot verts in extra virgin olive oil, added a bit of minced garlic, salt, and pepper.

She'd taken a couple of culinary classes and had developed a real love of cooking, but with no employment experience in the field, she'd decided to go for the sure thing and apply for a position as a waitress.

Chef James had been impressed with her skills and he'd talked to the owner about bringing her on as a line cook. Cathy had trembled with excitement. This opportunity had the potential to change her whole life.

She should go home and get some sleep so she would be well-rested for tomorrow, but she was just too keyed up.

Spying the bowling alley, she slowed and turned onto 72nd Street. She pulled into the parking lot and saw Brad standing near the front door. When she got out of her car, he walked over to her.

"Hey, sweet cheeks." He grinned.

His blue eyes glittered, sending her the unmistakable message that he was happy to see her, and her insides churned as she smiled.

Brad stopped just inches from her, leaned his hip against the door, and crossed his arms over his chest. Then he murmured, "God was just showing off when he made you."

The compliment tickled her. It was crazy how he could make her melt in her sandals with a sultry look and a few well-ordered words. That's the way she'd reacted to him since back in middle school.

They stood in the parking lot catching up, flirting, laughing, and teasing. Cathy told him about her opportunity at the restaurant. And they'd talked about careers and plans and dreams for the future.

At one point, he'd said, "Tell me again why we aren't dating."

She laughed and her thoughts scrambled like broken

eggs and all she could think to do was repeat, "Why aren't we dating?"

They weren't on some pre-planned romantic date. They weren't in some fancy restaurant. They were simply standing under the stars, in a dimly lit parking lot of a bowling alley. And there was no place else she'd rather be. Brad made her feel happy. He made her feel pretty. He made her feel good about herself.

When she realized how late it was, she told him she had to go, and he asked her to drop him off at the boardwalk on her way home.

"I know it's out of your way, but..."

"No problem." She'd waved off his concern. "Let me run inside to use the restroom. I'm going to grab a soda. You want anything?"

"Nah, I'm good. I'll just wait here."

While she was inside the bowling alley, she hoped he would ask her out. A chance at a new career as a line cook and another crack at the elusive Bradley Henderson. This was turning out to be a red letter day.

She pushed her way outside and saw him leaning over and talking to a group of kids inside a Mustang. His back was to her, so he didn't see her exit the building.

The words he spoke to someone in the car carried on

still night air. "Aside from being cute, what do you do for a living?"

Cathy's steps slowed, and that's when the realization hit her like an unexpected palm against the cheek, and it smarted something awful. Brad made all the girls feel happy. He made us all feel pretty. He made us all feel good about ourselves. It was the game he played, a game he'd mastered. And it worked out very well for him.

That game had always worked out well for him. How could she have forgotten that?

Tomorrow could become a changing day for her. She was about to embark on what could be a new phase in her life, a new direction. She was going after what might turn out to be a whole new career. A real, honest-to-goodness adult profession. She could work her way up. Earn the title of head chef someday. Maybe run a kitchen all on her own. Maybe own her own restaurant.

Did she really want to continue to do this? Brad was gorgeous, yes. He'd be a great catch. But...

"Hold on a sec," she heard him say. And then he turned to see her; he jogged over to her. "Hey," he said, "I can save you some time. Bobby and some of his friends are headed to the boardwalk. I'm going to hitch a ride with them, okay?"

"Sure. That's great."

His blue gaze grew intense and his voice lowered as he said, "I'll see you around, though, right?"

A vague smile was plastered on her face. He really was gorgeous. And he would be an amazing catch for someone. But would he ever be willing to be caught?

How long was she willing to play these stupid games?

"You bet," she told him.

The quick kiss he planted on her mouth startled her. As she watched him lope toward the car, she had this feeling that tonight had turned momentous. She felt suddenly pensive, ambivalent, as if she were standing on a precipice of some sort. The past held the familiar ground behind her, and the future was... out there... somewhere. And to find it, she'd have to turn her back on all the old, stymieing things and step blindly into the thin air.

Cathy got up from the chair and went to stand at the foot of Brad's hospital bed. He seemed so peaceful, so relaxed, but who knew what was happening inside his head. The bleeding had stopped, yes, but what damage had it done?

"I have every expectation that he'll wake up," the doctor had assured her earlier in the evening.

And she'd been so grateful to pass on that news to Brad's parents before they'd boarded their flight.

Her life had gone in a completely different direction after that night she and Brad had flirted for their final time as teens in the bowling alley parking lot. The next day had been her first as a paid, professional cook in an honest-to-goodness restaurant. And on her very first shift, she'd met Todd Kirkland, a produce supplier from Baltimore and the man she thought would bring her a lifetime of bliss.

God, had she been wrong.

Oh, her relationship with Todd had started out wonderfully. She'd been so full of hope. She wondered when, exactly, her happiness had turned to misery. The transformation had been so subtle at first that she had barely been aware of the change taking place. But over the course of the next nine years, her life had become a nightmare that had left her beaten and broke in every sense of those words—physically, emotionally, and financially.

After returning to Ocean City, it had taken over a year for her to get over her horrible experiences with her ex to the point that she'd felt safe dating again. She wouldn't have even then, except for the urging, nagging really, of Heather and Sara. When she'd lifted her head out of those dark gray clouds, Brad had been standing there like a beam of bright sunlight. Warm. Fun. Tantalizing. Cathy remembered Brad as being a master at the game of romance, so she'd been determined to keep their relationship playful and flirty. She'd been absolutely certain that's the way he'd want it; besides, with what she'd experienced with her ex, light and fun had been all she'd wanted, all she could handle.

The pristine white sheet covering Brad rippled in the dim light, snapping her out of her melancholic reflections. He'd moved.

His eyes remained closed and he was utterly still. But she was certain he'd shifted his foot a little. She pressed her fingers to her lips, torn between racing for the nurse and calling out to him so he would wake up. The need to learn that he hasn't suffered any permanent damage because of her foolishness nearly overwhelmed her, but rushing the process would be wrong.

The hinges on the door protested with a soft squeak. Cathy turned and forced a smile on her mouth when she saw Mr. and Mrs. Henderson. She hadn't seen them for nearly a year when they'd come to Ocean City for a short visit last summer.

"Hi, Cathy," Brad's father whispered. He set the newspaper he'd been carrying on a nearby table. "Thank you so much for staying with him."

Brad's mom enveloped her in a tight hug. "We flew into Philly, and as soon as we learned we couldn't get a puddle jumper to Ocean City until tomorrow, we decided to rent a car and drive. That got us here quicker. The nurse just gave us an update, hon." She leaned back, her hands still on Cathy's upper arms. "You look exhausted. We really appreciate your being here, Cathy."

Without even taking the time to greet them properly, she blurted out, "He moved. I need to go tell the nurse."

"Oh, thank heavens," Mrs. Henderson breathed. "Maybe he's about to wake up?"

"I don't know," Cathy admitted. "I really think I should go get the nurse."

Before she could move, a nurse who looked to be all of fourteen bustled into the room, a frown furrowing her brow. "Do you realize it's three o'clock in the morning? You need to keep it down in here. Patients are sleeping. Why are there three of you in here? Rules are rules. Two visitors. Period. One of you has to—"

"He moved," Cathy told her, and as soon as she spoke the words, Brad slid his hand from his side to his chest.

As if their gazes were powerful magnets and his body was made of iron, all four of them swiveled their heads toward the bed.

"I'm going to go call the doctor." The nurse pointed at Cathy. "You, come with me."

Following the nurse to the station just a few yards up the hallway, Cathy pleaded her case. "Listen, I've been here all day waiting for him to wake up. Don't make me leave just yet. I'll be quiet. I'll stand in one corner of the room. No one will know I'm there. I need to know that he's okay."

Completely ignoring Cathy, the nurse picked up the phone and spent all of fifteen seconds talking to someone on the other end of the line. As soon as she hung up, she directed her gaze at Cathy.

"I know you're worried," she said. "I wish I could accommodate you. I really do. But I already received a verbal warning this week for being lax on the visitation rules. The doctor is on his way, the floor nurse—*my boss*—will be by any moment.

You cannot be in that room while those other people are in there. Go to the waiting area at the end of the hall. Please." She pulled a chart from its slot, set it on the desktop, and then she began jotting some notes on the forms.

Rather than doing as she'd been told, Cathy hovered around the nurses' station and slowly moseyed over to the door of Brad's room. She didn't cross the threshold and figured that was close enough to be called following orders.

The sound of his voice caused her body to flush with relief.

"Mom? Dad? What are you doing here? Are you okay? What's going on?"

Bewilderment gave his words a blurry, rounded-edge sound.

"Everything's okay," his mother assured him.

"Where's Cathy?"

"Here," she called from the doorway. "I'm right here."

His blue eyes found hers just as the doctor brushed past her.

"Hi, Mr. Henderson. It's good to see you awake. I'm Doctor Jenkins. I'm on-call tonight. How are you doing?" The doctor addressed Brad as he approached the bed. "Do you have a headache? Can you tell me what year it is?"

"Yeah," Brad murmured. But instead of answering, he looked over at Cathy. "Are you okay?"

She nodded, emotion churning in her chest. There was so much she needed to say to him.

He took in the bandage on her arm. "You don't look okay."

"I'm fine." Then she added, "I promise." The last thing he should be doing was worrying about her.

Doctor Jenkins clapped his palms together and rubbed them vigorously in an attempt to capture everyone's attention. "I'm going to have to ask all of you fine folks to step out of the room for a bit. I need to do a thorough assessment, and then, Mr. Henderson, we're going to be sending you downstairs for a follow up MRI."

Brad's parents were ushered out of the room in a single file since Cathy refused to budge from the doorway.

"Go home," the doctor told her gently but firmly. "Get some sleep. Eat something. Come back in the morning."

For a split second, she considered darting

around him but then she'd only be causing a scene. In the end, the doctor would have his way, and that was totally as it should be.

Her gaze locked with Brad's for a few brief seconds. "I'm sorry," she mouthed. Her eyes watered, and before she could gauge his reaction, the doctor slowly closed the door in her face.

CHAPTER TWELVE

Cathy woke up to the trill of the spare cell phone Heather had lent her. She rolled to a sitting position, heavy-lidded and groggy, and glanced at the clock. Seven A.M. She'd fallen into bed three and a half hours ago, and now felt as if evil gnomes had slipped into her room during the wee hours and stuffed her head with cotton balls. Her stitched up arm ached like an abscessed tooth.

She picked up the phone and gave the screen a swipe.

Sara: Good morning, Auntie Cathy and Auntie Heather!

Heather: Oh, my goodness! Baby is here???

Sara: Yes! Over 2 hours ago.

Sara: Aaron Jackson.

Sara: Might call him AJ. Not sure yet.

Sara: Weighed in at 5 lbs 2 oz.

Sara: Everyone seemed happy with his weight.

Sara: Just under 4 wks early, the little bugger.

Cathy: Squeeee! Congrats! How do you feel?

Shrieking like an eight-year-old certainly wasn't on Cathy's to-do list at the moment, but Sara didn't have to know that. If there was ever a screech-worthy moment, this was it, no matter how lead-headed she might be feeling. A new baby called for going above and beyond.

Sara: Landon is sleeping about 5 yards away.

Sara: He was SO GOOD.

Sara: Labor hurt like a mother!

Sara: Not sure I want to do that again.

Sara: Ever.

Sara: Felt like I was pooping out a football.

Cathy: TMI! You seem a little keyed up.

Sara: Keyed up? Give me a break. I just performed a miracle. :)

Heather: I'll be in to hold that bundle of joy right after breakfast.

Heather: Tell us more.

Cathy: Yeah, how beautiful is he?

Sara: Prettier than an Ocean City sunrise.

Sara: He's breathing on his own.

Sara: We're going to try nursing in a bit. Doc is checking him over now.

Cathy: Let me shower and check on things at the café. Then I'll pop over to see our little miracle.

Heather: Cathy, want to ride over together?

Cathy: Can't. Need to catch up with Brad after.

Heather: Right.

Sara: Look you two. Landon told me about the accident.

Sara: Why didn't one of you tell me? >:(

Cathy: My fault. You didn't need more stress.

Sara: That's true. How is Brad?

Cathy: He woke up around 3 AM. Doc promptly kicked me out.

Cathy: His parents arrived. Drove down from Philadelphia airport.

Heather: Your arm?

Cathy: Okay. Need some ibuprofen. I'll be fine.

Sara: So you didn't talk to Brad?

Cathy: Not really. No time.

Heather: You'll talk to him today.

Cathy: IF he'll talk to me.

Sara: Why wouldn't he?

Cathy: Oh, I don't know.

Cathy: 'Cause I'm the bitch who rolled his jet ski? Put him in the hospital?

Heather: It was an accident.

Cathy: Yes. Caused by my recklessness.

She waited for one or the other of them to comment. Long seconds ticked by. Evidently, neither of them knew how to respond. Like bitter medicine, sometimes the truth was damned hard to swallow.

Sara: Hon, it'll be okay.

Heather: Just keep saying you're sorry.

"Will I ever learn to think before I act?" Cathy whispered right out loud.

Cathy: Getting in the shower.
Cathy: Later!

She tossed the phone on the mattress and headed toward the bathroom, tugging off her nightgown as she went.

* * *

A whole new shift of nurses had taken over the station since Cathy was last at the hospital. She smiled a hello as she passed by.

Holding AJ in the crook of her arm had been an amazing experience. The newborn's skin had felt as soft as velvet. He'd gazed up at her with dark, silent eyes, his tiny mouth pursed into a perfect bow. Cathy's heart ached with love.

She stopped at the threshold of Brad's hospital room and steeled herself. She had no idea what he might have to say. She sighed deeply, and then she rapped on the open door.

Brad sat on the edge of the bed, dressed in jeans and button down shirt.

Cathy didn't even try to hide her surprise. "You're being discharged?"

He nodded. "Seems that way. The MRI looked good. The pain meds took care of the headache. They couldn't find a reason to keep me. I called Mom and Dad this morning and they brought me some clean clothes. We've been waiting for a while for the discharge papers, so they went to search out some coffee for us."

The urge to rush at him, wrap her arms around him, was fierce, but she resisted.

"So you're really okay?"

Again, he nodded. "No heavy lifting for a while. And I'll have another scan next month. I'm going to be just fine. I had no idea I had any kind of malformation in my brain. But the doc doesn't think it'll cause me any problems."

No matter how hard she tried, she couldn't vanquish the guilt from her face.

"I'm going to be fine," he repeated.

Cathy winced. "Your poor jet ski isn't. It's probably totaled."

"Jack is going to take care of getting it back to the dock for me today." Then he pointed to her bandaged arm. "What's that?"

Absently, she fingered the gauze. "It's nothing.

A few stitches. I cut my arm on something in the water."

She went quiet, her brow pinching as she took her upper lip between her front teeth and glanced down at the floor. "Brad, I don't know if I can ever find the words to express how sorry I am for what happened."

When he didn't respond right away, she lifted her chin and found him studying her.

He asked, "I laid here for hours, going over and over what happened. You really thought I was going to hit you?"

"No." The word came out sounding firm and emphatic. "Absolutely not. You had nothing, or, um... very little to do with that... flinch."

She swallowed hard. She knew this man cared about her. Why did she find it so difficult to talk about this?

"I was angry," she told him. "I was feeling, um, constrained. Oppressed." She shook her head in frustration when neither of those words seemed exactly right.

"You're such a strong-willed woman," he murmured. "I can't imagine you ever allowing yourself to be oppressed." His gaze narrowed.

"What you yelled out was, 'Don't tell me what to do.'"

Cathy nodded. "Yeah. That feeling of being controlled, well, it churned up some..." She inhaled. "I got lost in the past for a minute. And then when you raised your arm and I cowered like that... I didn't even have time to think, Brad. I just acted. And then I was mortified by my own knee-jerk reaction, embarrassed because... Because it didn't have anything to do with you. I—I didn't feel threatened by you, is what I mean."

She knew she wasn't doing a very good job of explaining so she just stopped talking. Quiet hovered over them for quite some time.

"We've never talked much about your marriage." Brad pushed the tray table away from the bed so it wasn't between them, and he scooted to the edge of the mattress. "I know you went through some bad stuff with your ex. Just from some comments you've made. I've overheard you, Heather, and Sara refer to the guy using lots of—" his mouth twisted wryly "—colorful nicknames. But I never pressed you because I thought you would talk about it when you were ready. I knew you were pretty depressed when you came back to town, but I thought that was normal for someone going through a divorce. I also suspected that the relationship left you..." This time he pressed his lips into a fine line. "Financially burdened."

He reached up and raked his fingers through his hair. "But I never would have guessed that he'd been physically abusive. I had no idea."

The entire time he talked, her gaze very slowly slipped from his face to the floor. Then her chin lowered.

"Talking about this isn't easy," she whispered.

"I can imagine."

Thankfully, she didn't hear sympathy in his tone. She wouldn't have been able to stomach his pity.

Just do it. Just get the words out, and then it will be over.

"The abuse started very... subtly. I don't even think Todd was aware of what he was doing." Her voice went flat as she added, "He was always so apologetic. After, I mean. At first, anyway."

She shifted in the hard, plastic chair. "He was never happy with what I did. Always criticized my decisions. After a while, I began to question my reasoning, too. And he became smothering;

although, he made it seem like he loved me so much he couldn't be away from me. Before I realized it, I was contacting Grandmom less and less. I avoided calls from Heather and Sara, and I was seeing them almost never.

"I learned from my therapist—yes, I spent some time in therapy after the divorce—that this kind of gradual increase is what usually happens. The mental and emotional abuse. The isolation. Somehow, Todd had me believing I couldn't manage without him. I did try to assert myself, but I always ended up feeling belittled and, well, stupid."

Cathy glanced up at Brad, but the astonishment on his face forced her to look away.

"The first time he put his hands on me," she said, "he didn't actually hurt me. We'd gotten into an argument. About money. We fought about money a lot. I worked almost seven days a week. I earned a fairly good salary. But there was never any money in the checking account. Anyway, when I demanded to know what he was doing with our finances, he grabbed me. Shook me."

She paused, remembering how her head had jerked, how she'd felt like a rag doll, how that flash of fear had jolted her just as sharply as the shake had.

"It's not something that happened every week." She paused, licked her lips. "I can't even say it happened every month. But... it happened. And it didn't take long until I became... a completely different person. I think about that woman I became, and I can't even recognize her."

Cathy took a moment to close her eyes. Inhaling deeply, she pictured in her mind how she'd changed back then, how meek and compliant she'd become, and as her therapist had taught her, Cathy mentally hugged that woman, forgave her, told her she was safe, that everything was going to be all right.

"One summer, Heather and Sara kept bugging me to come visit them," she continued. "Todd refused to let me go. When I told him I wanted to see my friends, he backhanded me. Bruised my eye." She sighed. "I couldn't come to Ocean City with a black eye. I didn't want to lie about how it happened, so I decided it was best to stay home. I didn't want to worry them. I didn't want them telling my grandmother what was going on."

Something about Brad's exhalation drew her

attention. He sat there in silence, his jaw clenched, his fingers laced so tightly that the backs of his hands had gone pale.

"According to my therapist," she told him, "I conjured up all the classic reasoning, all the compelling rationale for staying with my abuser. He needs me. I can't cope without him. It'll get better. It won't happen again. I don't want my friends and family to know, to worry. If they find out, they'll only make things worse for me." She heaved another sigh. "It was a vicious cycle. A wildly spinning merry-go-round. And it never entered my little pea brain to just *get off the freakin' ride*."

"So what was it?"

Cathy looked up, frowning at his question. "I'm sorry?"

"What was it?" he repeated. "What caused you to leave?"

"Grandmom got sick." Her heart ached when she thought about that time in her life. "She didn't call me right away; she didn't call until she was so, so ill. She needed me come take care of her, but Todd would have none of it. He accused me of wanting to leave him." She shook her head. "He said vile things to me. And then he stopped talking and started punching."

She stood up and went to the window. "I don't really remember leaving Baltimore. I barely remember the drive to Ocean City. I showed up at home... at Grandmom's house with just the clothes on my back."

Brad got up from the bed and came around to stand behind her. She could sense the solid bulk of him even though their bodies weren't touching.

"How the hell did that happen to you?" he finally asked, soulful sorrow painting his words in heavy, dark hues.

She gave her shoulders a momentary lift. "My therapist thinks my childhood contributed to what she called my abuse mentality. The way I was raised the first seven or so years of my life. Living with a mother who was addicted to drugs, who was willing to do anything, suffer anything for her next fix. She was willing to put me in danger to get what she needed. I grew up feeling helpless. Unable to have any say in my circumstances or voice an opinion. Fending for myself. I often went to bed hungry. Often roamed the streets alone because I didn't know where my mom was. And then going from that to my Grandmother's house where the rules were so strict, and again, I had no say." She turned and faced him. "Who knew that would create such a perfect psychological storm for me to become an abused wife?"

Brad placed gentle hands on her shoulders.

"It took so long for me to feel any semblance of normal," she told him. "Todd utterly crushed me. I didn't think I'd survive it. I had skills in the kitchen, but I was sure no one would hire me. Don't ask me why. I don't have an answer for that. Todd left me with nothing. He'd borrowed against our house. He'd cleaned out the savings. He'd started several businesses that had failed. I learned he'd opened several lines of credit. Thank goodness, only one credit card was in both our names." She swiveled her head slowly back and forth, her mind entrenched in the awful past. "He even threatened to take half of my Grandmom's house." She looked up into Brad's blue eyes. "She was still alive at the time. She was so mad; she vowed to live until the divorce was final."

Brad smiled. "I always liked that feisty old woman."

"She almost made it, too," she said softly.

"Heather and Sara were my lifeline. I don't know what I'd have done without them. They helped me take care of Grandmom. They found a good divorce lawyer for me. He couldn't get anything out of Todd because you can't get water out of a rock, but he did keep Todd's grubby hands off Grandmom's house and the small bit of savings she left me." She reached up and hooked her fingers over Brad's forearm. "I used that money to start The Café. And making it a success became my passion. That first year, I barely broke even. But I never looked back." She let her fingers slip from his arm. "It's been the hardest thing... and the most satisfying thing I've ever done."

He took a step away from her and crossed his arms over his chest. "Like I said, I suspected you took a significant financial hit when you filed for divorce, but I never realized how hard a hit you took. Now I understand why you've been so concerned about me going into debt."

She cocked a curious brow but said nothing.

"You ragged out on me about it the first time you came to the arcade." He nodded slowly. "And then you accused me of asking you to marry me because I wanted you to pay off the mortgage on the place."

Cathy tilted her head a fraction. "I think what I said was you wanted me to *help* you pay off the mortgage."

He grinned. "Mere semantics."

"I remember you said you didn't owe a mortgage. How can that be? What are you? A magician?"

Taking in the twinkle in his eyes, she realized that the atmosphere between them had lost all semblance of the tension she'd felt upon entering the hospital room.

"I'll tell you all about that," he told her. "Later. Right now, there are more important things you need to hear."

She turned slightly, leaned her bottom against the low window sill, and waited.

"I have to take some responsibility for what happened out there on the bay," he told her. "I've wanted to talk to you about... us, about our relationship, for such a long time. But I hadn't because... well, because I was—" he gave a shrug "—scared of what you might say. Of what you would do. So when I did... broach the subject, I was frustrated. And annoyed. With you. With myself. With our situation. Which seemed, to me, to be going nowhere. And I obviously went about everything all wrong.

"Cathy," he continued, "I should have started out by telling you how I feel about you. I should have explained to you what you mean to me. I should have shared my vision for our future. I've been thinking about it for a long time."

He paused, licked his dusky lips, tilted his head, softened his tone. "I love you, Cathy. I do."

She felt her insides squirm and her gaze automatically drifted away from his face. But he reached out and captured her chin, gently guiding her gaze back to his.

"Don't do that. Don't put up those barriers. Don't shut me out. We know each other too well not to be completely honest here."

Her gaze roved over his handsome face. She couldn't deny that what he said was true.

"It's just that," she began, and then she stopped. After taking a deep breath, she tried again. "That word. It has..." She gently pushed his hand away from her face. "It has a lot of dark and murky emotions glommed onto it, in my experience."

Brad reached up and brushed her hair off her shoulder without actually touching her body.

"Sweetheart, what your ex showed you, how he treated you, that wasn't love."

She met his gaze, full on. "He thought it was."

"Well, he was wrong," Brad told her. "Dead wrong. And you know it's true."

After a moment, she admitted, "It's not just Todd. I loved my mother. I would have done anything for her. And when I think about all the precarious situations she put me in..." She let the rest of the thought fade as she shook her head. "It's frightening, Brad. And then there was Grandmom. I was so grateful to her for all she did for me. But her love had so many stipulations attached to it. I had to do what I was told, no questions asked. I ran from that as fast as I could." She muttered, "I jumped right out of that frying pan into the fire."

Inhaling deeply, she firmed her jaw. "My ideas of love are... twisted."

"I don't believe that," he said. "If you were truly ignorant of what love is, you wouldn't be able to so easily explain what it isn't."

She saw his hand lift, knew he wanted to touch her, but then he evidently changed his mind.

"You love Sara and Heather." Matter-of-factness shored up his tone. "You have loved them for as long as I've known you. You've helped them through all manner of bad times. When Sara lost Greg, you were there for her. When Heather was diagnosed with breast cancer, you practically moved in with her."

"And I paid a terrible price for it when I went home to Todd," she murmured. "But they needed me."

He nodded. "There's your proof. Simple and undeniable. You know what love is. And you know what it isn't."

She slipped her fingers into her pockets and lifted her shoulders. "It's more complicated than that, Brad."

"No," he disagreed. "It isn't."

He inched a little closer, but he was careful not to touch her. "You're driving me crazy. You smell like lemon and flowers, and I want to wrap my arms around you and kiss you until you can't breathe."

She smiled despite the discomfort she felt.

"But I can't. I won't." He sighed. "Not until you tell me how you feel. About me. About us."

In her mind, love was a difficult, bumpy subject that never failed to trip up the emotions like an unexpected rise in the pavement that caused an ugly pratfall. She wasn't interested in taking that kind of nosedive ever again, but it seemed Brad didn't intend to let this go.

"You smiled," he said. "That has to be a good sign."

"I smiled because I like it when you say I drive you crazy. It makes me feel good."

"And..." He waved his hand in a circling motion, urging her to go on.

"Brad." Reluctance drew out his name and conveyed her aversion, and his reaction was immediate. His mouth flattened and his shoulders squared as if he were preparing himself for bad news.

"Okay," she began, "you want honesty, I'll give you honesty. No one makes me feel like you do. No one. You make me happy. I smile more when I'm with you than I have in a very long time. I love being with you. I care so much about you." She clasped her hands together, closed her eyes, and when she opened them, she scrutinized his handsome face in silence as she battled the fear in her heart. Then she quietly admitted, "I love you. I do love you."

"There." He stepped toward her, slid his arms around her. "Was that so hard?"

"Wait."

Her flattened palm pressing against his chest took him aback.

"I'm not finished." She lifted her chin. "I am *not* going to marry you, Brad. Ever."

Movement at the door had both of them swiveling their heads.

Brad's parents stood inside the room, and Cathy felt her face grow hot as fire as she wondered how much they had overheard. Dismay pulled at Mrs. Henderson's lovely face.

"We only brought three cups of coffee," Mr. Henderson blustered to cover the awkwardness. "Maybe we should go buy another cup."

"That won't be necessary," Cathy assured him. "I have to get back to the café. I just popped in to check on Brad."

The next few minutes were spent exchanging clumsy niceties. Finally, Cathy said her good-byes, and glanced at Brad. "I'll talk to you later?"

But the disappointment reflecting in his gaze had two words ringing through her head.

Or not.

CHAPTER THIRTEEN

Cathy traced the pads of her fingers over the little cherub's bald head, smiling at the warm silkiness beneath her touch. Yes, his name was Aaron, but he'd always be *the little cherub* in Cathy's mind. She imagined him through the years—on his first day of elementary school, in his cap and gown at his high school graduation, in some impressive military uniform, in a tux at his wedding—and she would be there teasing him with the angelic nickname. It would drive him nuts with embarrassment. She chuckled.

"What are you laughing at over there?" Heather asked her.

Since Sara came home from the hospital, the three friends had made an effort to gather together late each afternoon at Sara's house. Snuggling with the baby filled Cathy's heart near to bursting with adoration. He was such a comfort to her.

"Just thinking of ways I'm going to tease this little one," Cathy said.

Delivered at just under thirty-seven weeks, Aaron remained in the hospital for a few extra days so the medical staff could keep a close watch on him. But, tiny miracle that he was, he amazed everyone with his strength and vitality. His heart rate and breathing patterns were in the normal range. His oxygen saturation remained high. He breastfed like a pro, and he maintained a stable body temperature, so the doctors were very pleased to release him. Sara and Landon watched him like sharp-eyed hawks, logging his feedings, his sleep, even his diaper changes.

Eventually, the new parents would relax, but Cathy understood their vigilance. The little cherub was downright teeny, and when he worked himself up, he became a miniature prize fighter, complete with a fierce and wrinkled face and itty-bitty fists.

Right now, though, he snoozed contentedly, nestled in the crook of Cathy's neck.

"Have you heard from him?" Sara asked Cathy.

It was a question either Sara or Heather asked her every day.

"No," she said. "It's been almost two weeks. He hasn't called. He hasn't stopped into the café for coffee. I think we all have to come to the conclusion that he's made his intentions clear."

"You don't know that," Heather chimed in. "Could it be that you haven't seen him in the café because he hasn't been cleared to go back to work on the beach patrol?"

Cathy nodded, her jaw sliding against the baby's warm, fuzzy head. "Sure, that could very well be true. But he could call," she pointed out. "He banged his head when he fell off the jet ski. As far as I know, his fingers are working just fine."

The quip fell flat and guilt welled in her chest; she wondered if she'd ever be able to think about or mention the accident without being walloped by remorse.

Sara came over and fiddled with the little cotton cloth beanie that Aaron wore. "Don't be such a fatalist. Landon's been working some long hours with Brad at the arcade. According to Landon, Brad's been pushing the crew he hired really hard, and Brad's dad was there helping, too. So maybe he hasn't called you because he's busy."

Cathy didn't argue, she sat there basking in the unexpected gratitude that suddenly permeated her being. She looked from Sara to Heather and back again.

"You know," she told them, "I have never been happier to be ganged up on by you two."

The now-repaired rift between Heather and Cathy had shifted their relationship a bit. They were a little more cautious with their words, a little more appreciative of their friendship. Cathy knew this walking-on-eggshells phase wouldn't last long, and soon they'd be back to razzing the dickens out of each other. But for now she intended to respect the peaceful period for the simple fact that she wanted Heather to understand just how delighted she was that things between them were once again amiable.

She had missed being with Sara and Heather as a threesome. Terribly.

Her phone trilled with a text, and although the little cherub started, he didn't wake.

"Well, speak of the devil," Cathy murmured, juggling her phone with one hand.

Brad: Can you come to the arcade at 7 PM?

She thought a moment before responding. Heather read the text over her shoulder.

"I hope you don't mind my nosiness," Heather murmured.

"Not a bit." Cathy grinned as she began tapping in a response with one thumb.

Cathy: Well, my legs are working so I guess I can.

Heather gasped. "Cathy, do you really think being a smartass is the way to go? I mean, we've been waiting to hear from Brad—"

Cathy chuckled, feeling suddenly light-headed

as she pressed the send button. Then she looked up at Heather. "*We've* been waiting?"

"Okay, okay." Heather lifted her hand like a traffic cop. "You've been waiting."

"The hell with that," Sara said, scooping up Aaron and cradling him in her arms. "Heather is right. We've been waiting for almost two weeks for this. You be nice, darn it."

"I'm being me," Cathy stated with a shrug. "I can't be anybody else."

Both Heather and Sara shared a look, both exhaling audibly.

Brad: WOULD you come to the arcade?
Cathy: Sure. See you at 7.

"Well—" she stood and tugged at the hem of her t-shirt, nerves twitching in her extremities "—the moment of truth is upon us. Things between us are either going to remain the same..." She pressed her palm to her stomach. "Or they're not."

"Let's talk about what you're going to wear," Heather said.

And Cathy grinned.

The three women stood so close they could

almost reach out and touch each other. In that moment, Cathy felt enormously blessed. True friendship could withstand the fiercest storms. They were her sisters; with them, she laughed a little louder, cried a little less, and smiled a whole lot more. Sara and Heather were the kind of friends who could hear her... even when she was silent. They lectured her when she needed it, and even when she didn't. And she was always quick to return that favor. But she didn't dare voice any of these thoughts because they were also the kind of friends who would tease her into next week for that kind of sap.

* * *

The mini golf course had been completely transformed. The dinosaurs sported a fresh coat of paint and the landscaping looked neat and tidy. The green fabric inside the putting areas had been replaced. Even the fencing surrounding the course had been repaired and painted. All the signage looked brand new, as well.

Brad came out of the front door of the arcade just as she reached it.

"The place looks great," she told him, turning to look out over the course. "You'll be opening soon, it looks like."

He nodded, and she noticed that he was carrying two golf clubs.

"I've booked some Grand Opening advertising for next week." He balanced the head of the clubs on the ground and cupped his palm over the top of the handles. "I still have a few things to do inside, but it's coming together much faster than I expected. I'm going to put off the food counter for a while. Just see how it goes."

"Well, I'm happy to help with that if…"

"I appreciate that," he said. "I do. But I got to talking to my dad about it, and I realized that my plans were a little…" He chuckled. "Overblown, I guess you could say. I need to take it nice and slow if I want to succeed. And I do."

The light at the corner changed, and cars and SUVs out on Coastal Highway slowed to a stop. Cathy hadn't realized how loud the sounds of traffic had been until they had quieted.

Finally, she said, "So you never did tell me."

His tawny brows arched.

"How you got the place," she finished.

His sexy mouth split into a wide grin. "I inherited it."

The next few minutes were spent talking about billionaire Howard Hopewell, how he'd seen Brad as a teen in the documentary that was filmed about the Ocean City Beach Patrol.

"The one that gave birth to Putt-putt?"

"The very one."

The story of Hopewell amazed Cathy. "So this guy left you a business, but you didn't save his life?"

"I didn't save *his* life," Brad told her. "But I've saved a lot of lives. According to the letter his lawyer sent me, Mr. Hopewell felt my enthusiasm for the job deserved to be recognized."

"And it does." She slipped her car key into her back pocket. "And I want to apologize if I ever made you feel—"

"Don't," he said, gently cutting her off. "You never made me feel anything I didn't want to feel."

But she refused to acquiesce. "I've teased you about your job as a life guard, Brad. And I shouldn't have."

"And I've teased you," he insisted, "about practically everything. It's what we do. It's how we *are*. It's what works for us. If others don't like it, tough." He stared at her for a moment. "Right?"

She wasn't sure what this meant. It sounded like he was willing to let their relationship go on as it had. Or it could mean he only wanted to keep parts of it.

"So." She tilted her head as she drew out the word. "Does this mean we're okay?"

He smiled, and her insides began to do that odd butterfly flutter.

"Of course, we're okay," he told her. "We've always been okay, right?"

"The way you keep asking," she murmured, "I'm not sure you're all that sure."

The sound of his low laughter set off a chain reaction in her body. Her pulse throbbed to life, her breath quickened, her temperature notched up a degree.

"You know me too well." He offered her one of the golf clubs. "Come on. Let's play a round."

"Of putt-putt? Gosh, I feel like we're back in high school, Brad," she teased, but she took the club from him.

"We can play and... talk a little bit."

She narrowed her eyes. "Why does that plan make me a tad suspicious?"

"That's probably a healthy thing."

He led her through the leafy hedges onto the course.

"You go first," he said. "I've already teed up your ball."

"Well, now weren't you confident?"

"Actually, I was," he admitted softly.

Cathy loved this playful banter. It made her feel impish. Sexy. *Wanted.* Brad was good at it. An expert, actually, and that's one of the reasons she loved him. She found his confidence appealing. She loved that he could show such self-assurance yet never come off as cocky.

"The truth is," he told her, "the course was just completed today. I wanted you to be the first to tee off."

Syrupy sweet emotion filled her chest as she straddled the ball.

"Don't expect much," she warned. "I can't even remember the last time I played."

She looked down the green at the hole and made a mental measure of how hard she should swing. She tapped the ball and then held her breath as it traveled along the alleyway. The ball rolled straight for the hole, but slowed to a crawl. It hovered on the edge, but then dropped out of sight with a satisfying *thunk*.

Cathy let out a shout of triumph and jumped onto the balls of her feet. Brad reared back his head and laughed.

"That is unbelievable!" He took two giant steps and enveloped her in a hug.

He smelled like a summertime walk in the woods. She knew it hadn't been all that long since they'd touched, but it felt like a lifetime.

"It's got to be good luck, right?" he asked. "For the arcade, I mean. This is a sign that things are going to go well."

"I hope so." She went to retrieve her ball while he teed up.

"Listen," he said as he eyed the ball and the hole to line up his shot, "my mom asked me a question about our relationship that had me doing some heavy duty thinking."

"You talked with your mom about us?"

"My dad was in on the discussion, too." He hit the ball, and it rolled toward the hole, stopping several inches short of its goal.

"Well, they overheard you say you were never going to marry me." He lined up his second shot. "I had to tell them something."

"I guess you did."

Brad tapped the ball and it dropped into the hole.

"I told them about the on-again-off-again thing we have going," he continued. "And how I continued to go along with it even when I wanted more out of the relationship."

He bent and picked up his ball. He straightened, his blue eyes latching onto hers. "Mom asked me why. Why, she wanted to know, would I go along with a thing like that if that's not what I wanted. So I started thinking. It took me *days*, but I think I've got it worked out."

"Oh?"

"You're up." Planting his hand at her lower back, he gently guided her to the tee area of the second hole.

Cathy positioned her ball in the small painted circle.

"I was willing to give you the time you needed," he said. "Time to celebrate your newfound freedom. Time to enjoy your friends. Time to clear out the residual impact of your ex. Shake off the dust, so to speak."

"There was a blanket of dust," she muttered.

"You needed time to restore your confidence. And reconnect with, I don't know, who you are and what you want. Divorce does a number on people. You needed to come to terms with any betrayal issues or abandonment issues you might have."

It took her four attempts to get the ball into the hole, and then he moved into position at the head of the green. With his focus on the ball, he said, "You needed time to re-establish your sexual sovereignty." He waggled his head as he added, "And I was happy to help facilitate that whenever you needed me."

Cathy groaned. "Please tell me you didn't tell your mother that last bit."

"I didn't tell her any of this. She merely asked the question, and she left it up to me to figure out an answer. But it turned out to be a good exercise, don't you think?"

He whacked the ball and it skidded along and dropped neatly into the hole.

She raised her arms and yelled out. "Whoa! We

both have a hole in one." She twisted her mouth to the side. "Maybe we should stop now."

"No way," he told her. "We have to keep going."

Cathy stepped onto the third green.

"Where was I?" he asked.

"You proclaimed my need for sexual sovereignty." She pointed her club at him. "Which, I might add, you have facilitated expertly."

"Thank you." He offered a small bow of his head.

Looking down the curvy alleyway, Cathy said, "I think I might need some help lining up this shot."

Brad moved behind her, reaching around her to slide his hands overtop hers on the club. They straddled the ball, and Cathy arched her back, shifted from one foot to the other, which made her bottom wiggle a little.

She grinned and glanced over her shoulder. "Is that a trophy in your pocket, or are you just happy to see me?"

His breath was warm against her neck as he released a sexy chuckle. "Cathy, I'm trying to be serious here."

"You're trying to be something," she teased.

He planted a kiss on her jaw. "Try to focus, would you?"

"Yes, sir."

"So as I was saying," he continued smoothly, as he helped guide her swing. "I think what I've been doing is giving you the space and the time you need to overcome your past, to feel empowered, to learn to trust yourself and others—meaning me, hopefully—so you can leave the past behind and be fully present when we're together."

Cathy smacked the ball and watched as it hit the side wall twice before disappearing into the hole. She squealed like a gleeful toddler, dropped the club, and spun to face Brad. She hopped into his arms and wrapped her legs around his waist. He cupped her bottom, and she pressed her palms on either side of his handsome face.

"This is so fun!" She smiled at him. "People are going to *love* this place."

Then she kissed him, hard; his mouth was warm and wet and tasted faintly of mint.

She pulled back and gazed deeply into his eyes. "You are an amazing man. You're smart, funny, and sexy as hell. If there wasn't traffic whizzing by out there, I'd rip off your clothes and have my way with you right here. You're just what I need, Brad

Henderson. And I love you. I think I've loved you for a long, long time."

Appreciation gleamed in his azure eyes.

"But don't think for a minute that you have me fooled. Residual impact, betrayal and abandonment issues, restoring self-confidence." She snorted. "Re-establish sexual sovereignty? There is no way you came up with that crap on your own. You've been googling. Hard. Admit it."

His mouth quirked at one corner and he quipped, "Like I said, you know me so well. That's one of the reasons why I love you."

Cathy slid out of his arms, their gazes remaining connected, growing more somber.

"I know we don't say that often enough," she confessed. "That's something we should work on, maybe?"

"Definitely."

Earnestness leveled her tone even further. "Brad, I need to know... are you really okay with us not getting married? Are we on the same page here?"

He gave an easy nod. "Kind of."

She stared at him until he physically placed his hands on her shoulders and turned her around.

"Go get your ball. It's my turn."

Cathy should have known something was up when he didn't move to tee up; he just stood there watching her. She cast a suspicious glance at him as she made her way toward the far end of the green—and she promptly ran into something dangling from an overhead tree branch. Sure it was a spider or some other creepy-crawly, she let out a squeal and batted the air.

"Bug!" she cried out when she felt it hit her a second time.

"It's not a bug." Brad jogged toward her, laughing. "I'm sorry. It wasn't supposed to happen like that."

"What wasn't...?" She stopped and went still while he reached to free whatever had become entangled in her hair.

"Does *anything* we do happen like it's supposed to?" she asked.

"Not very often. But that's why we're so good together, right?"

"Why do you keep doing that? Turning your statements into questions."

"Don't move. I almost have it," he whispered. "I keep asking because I want you to feel like you have a say. I never want to make you feel, um, trapped."

If he hadn't told her not to move, she'd have swung around and hugged him tightly. He was too sweet for words.

"Like this bug stuck in my hair?" she teased.

"I was thinking more along the lines of how you felt... when you were with your mom. With your grandmother. With your ex. I never want to make you feel... confined." His tone lightened as he said, "Like I told you, it's not a bug." He pulled away. "Here."

Her eyes went wide when she saw the object in his fingers. "A *ring*? An *engagement* ring?" She inched backward. "Damn it, Brad—"

"It's not an engagement ring."

The blue stone glistening in the sunlight caught her attention, and she blinked. "It's lapis." Her voice went soft and a frown bit into her brow.

"The jeweler told me that lapis has healing qualities," he said. "It's thought to boost self-confidence and inner power."

"You think I need more of that, do you?" she murmured. Her bewilderment over why he was giving her a ring must have continued to shadow her expression.

"Cathy, I need some sort of commitment from you. I'm not talking about a marriage certificate. But I do need something that signifies we're a... *thing*. I don't need a vow." He tilted his head. "But I do need a promise."

"This is a promise ring?" She stood there a moment, and then she fought the smile that tugged at her mouth. "We *are* back in high school, aren't we?"

"Stop," he said. "Don't make fun of me." But then he grinned too, shrugging. "I thought it was a good idea. For both of us. Am I being stupid?"

She shook her head. "No. You're being romantic." Then she lifted her hand, palm up. "Give me the ring," she groused. "If you need a promise, I'll give you a promise." She slipped it onto her finger and took a moment to look at it.

"It's beautiful," she told him.

The intense blue of the square semi-precious stone was flecked with gold and polished to a high-gloss shine.

"When I came home like a whipped puppy," she said, "my grandmother kept assuring me that, eventually, everything would be okay. That the divorce would be hard, but there would be a better life for me afterward. That I wouldn't be alone forever. I wasn't so sure because, well, I felt so damned broken, you know? But Grandmom kept on insisting. Months later after she'd passed and I ventured out for the first time, I'd found a card she'd given me. She'd left me a piece of very good advice. *'Fall in love when you're ready, Cathy,'* she'd written, *'not when you're lonely.'*"

Thoughts wrapped around her like a velvety cloak, soft and warm, and when she finally lifted her gaze to Brad's, she saw that his eyes were filled with emotion too.

"Because of you, I haven't been lonely," she told him. "Because of you, I feel like I've been put back together, that my jagged edges have been filed down, smoothed over." She smiled into his handsome face. "Because of you, Brad, I'm more than ready to fall in love. And I guess that's a good thing because you already have my heart."

"I'll take care of it." He cupped her jaw in his palm. "And that's a promise I intend to prove."

He slipped his arms around her and pulled her to

him, and Cathy knew that, although the love they shared might be unconventional, it was forever.

EPILOGUE

Late afternoon sunlight cast a golden autumnal glow across the sand. Ocean waves offered pleasant background music. A warm, light breeze fluttered the gauzy fabric that decorated the pristine white archway that had been planted in the sand. A lush flower arrangement sat on the small table that had been positioned under the arch. White folding chairs were lined up in two short rows, but few of them would be in use as most of the attendees would be participating in the ceremony in some way.

Cathy lingered on the apex of the dune, watching the street for guests to arrive, glancing occasionally at the lovely ceremonial set up waiting on the beach, and taking every opportunity to admire her bouquet of white roses and daisies. Just as she buried her nose in the lusciously scented flowers, Brad came up behind her. His lips were warm and possessive on her neck, and a delicious shiver coursed along the curve of her shoulder.

"Jack says he's ready," Brad murmured against her hair. "All he needs is the bride and groom."

"He did a lovely job of decorating."

"With the hundreds of beach weddings he's planned over the years..." Brad planted another sweet kiss on the top of Cathy's bare shoulder. "He could get the job done with both hands tied behind his back."

"Hmm." Distracted by the silky touch of his lips on her skin, by the brush of his warm breath on her temple, she leaned her head to the side, offering him more. And he didn't disappoint her. Her nipples budded to life, ached to be touched, and she slowly filled her lungs with salt-tinged air and dragged her eyelids open. "That feels wonderful."

She could feel him grin against her neck.

"Are you sure you're not going to break out in hives today?" he asked.

Cathy turned to face him, reaching up to encircle his neck with her arms. "Hives?" she asked, kissing his chin lightly and pressing her breasts against his chest.

His hands at the small of her back, he pulled her closer until their naughty bits snuggled, separated by mere layers of fabric.

"You know," he whispered, and then tilted his head to indicate the arch and makeshift altar that he and Jack had arranged out on the beach. "The wedding."

"Ah." Her brows rounded. "I'll be fine. It's bridal gowns I'm allergic to, not bridesmaid dresses."

A couple hours later, Cathy stood back from the happy group, taking it all in. Sara and Landon's wedding had been simple and perfect. From the moment she'd arrived, Sara had radiated sheer bliss. Her white, full-skirted sundress struck her at mid-calf, and she'd traipsed along the sandy aisle unapologetically barefoot. She'd never looked more beautiful. Emotion had moistened her eyes as she'd spoken her vows. Geneva looked lovely in her mother-of-the-bride dress, and she beamed with happiness as she'd sat holding two-month-old Aaron. Like the perfect little cherub he was, the baby had slept through the whole affair. Landon's sister and brother-in-law had flown into town with their two children to attend the ceremony, and judging from their broad smiles as they congratulated the newlyweds, it seemed that their family troubles had been worked out.

Heather looked stunning, more from sheer joy than anything else, as she and Daniel huddled near the decorated arch. Mia's shyness hadn't kept her from performing her duties as flower girl; now she hovered near her father and Heather, her chin lifted with pride, her now-empty basket hanging from her arm.

Seeing Sara and Heather so happy filled Cathy's heart near to bursting. Those two women meant the world to her. They were her family. Her sisters-of-the-heart. The three of them were comfortable together, in good times and in bad, in the chatter of everyday life, and even in life's more quiet times. She loved them, would move heaven and earth to help them, and she knew they would do the same for her.

And then Cathy's gaze landed on Brad as he walked across the sand toward her. The suit he wore accentuated his golden good looks. His gorgeous smile and perfectly positioned dimples left her utterly breathless, but it was his patience and his understanding that won her trust and captured her heart. She loved this man, deeply, intensely, profoundly. He was everything she needed and more. It might have taken her a while to figure it out, but he was truly the love of her life.

He reached out and tipped up her chin with a gentle touch of his index finger and kissed her—a silent token of his affection—and she held his gaze for a long moment, in answer. It was a move that had become a habit over the weeks that had passed since she'd accepted his promise ring. Every time she looked at that ring, she grinned. The piece of jewelry was the perfect representation of their relationship, serious and intimate, yet also light and fun and playful.

"I think they're ready to head up to The Lonely Loon for champagne," he told her.

"And dinner," she quipped. "I'm starved."

He leaned closer. "I'm looking forward to dessert, myself."

Desire curled in her belly and she suspected his reference had nothing to do with food.

"That'll have to wait until later." She wrapped an arm around his waist as they walked and breezily said, "If you play your cards right, you just might get me to do this one day."

He stopped in his tracks. "What? *Really?*"

Her throaty chuckle was carried away on the sea breeze. She loved keeping this man on his toes.

* * *

Thank you for reading *WILD HEARTS OF SUMMER*. If you enjoyed this book, please consider leaving a review. Good reviews help new readers find Donna's books. Please tell your friends about The Ocean City Boardwalk Series. Word of mouth is the best advertisement an author can get!

Would you like to know more about the rift between Cathy and Heather? Learn exactly what happened in *TWO HEARTS IN WINTER*, Book 2 of the Ocean City Boardwalk Series.

Keep scrolling to read a note from the author

and also several delicious recipes that Cathy mentions in the book.

A Note From the Author

Living on the beach, I have witnessed some wondrous things: pods of dolphins swimming along the coast, whales blowing seawater high into the air, even a giant manta ray soaring out of the ocean. But my favorite pastime is people watching. I am inspired by young lovers walking hand in hand, or frolicking in the waves, or sitting on the sand with their heads together. These romantic sights make me want to create characters and conjure stories.

I hope you enjoyed Cathy and Brad's story. If you did, I'd like to suggest you look for the other titles in the Ocean City Boardwalk Series. Interested in the other titles in The Inheritance Series? Click here.

I love to interact with readers, so let's keep in touch. I send out a monthly newsletter to announce sales, giveaways, and new releases. I award prizes in each issue. Sign up so you don't miss your chance to win a gift card or a free book.

Keep scrolling for some delicious recipes!

Love and Light,
Donna

Blueberry Pancakes

Ingredients:

1 egg

1 cup all-purpose flour

1 cup milk

2 tablespoons vegetable oil

2 tablespoon sugar

3 teaspoon baking powder

1/2 teaspoon salt

1 pint fresh blueberries, picked over, washed, and dried

Directions:

1. Whisk the egg until fluffy. Add the flour, milk, oil, sugar, baking powder, and salt and beat just until smooth. Gently stir in

blueberries, being careful not to mash the fruit.

2. Spray a frying pan with cooking spray and heat over medium flame. Once the pan is hot, pour about 3 tablespoons of batter into the pan. Cook pancake until puffed in the center and dry around the edges. Flip the pancake and cook the other side until golden brown.

3. Keep pancakes warm in a 250°F oven until all pancakes are cooked. Serve with butter and maple syrup.

Lemon Ricotta Pancakes with Lemon Curd and Raspberries

Ingredients:

    1 cup all-purpose flour

    1 tablespoon baking powder

    1/4 teaspoon cinnamon

    1/2 teaspoon salt

    2 tablespoon sugar

    1 cup whole milk ricotta cheese

    2 eggs

    2/3 cup milk

    1 large lemon, zested and juiced

    1 11-ounce jar of lemon curd

    1/2 pint of fresh raspberries

Directions:

Lemon Ricotta Pancakes with Lemon Curd and Raspberries

1. In a small bowl, stir together the flour, baking powder, cinnamon, salt, and sugar. In a large bowl, whisk together the ricotta cheese, eggs, milk, lemon juice, and zest. Whisk the dry ingredients into the wet ingredients until just combined. Do not over mix.

2. Spray a frying pan with non-stick spray and heat the pan over medium heat. Add 1/4 cup of batter to the hot pan and cook until puffed in the center and dry around the edges. Flip and cook other side. Keep pancakes warm in a 250°F oven until all pancakes are cooked.

3. Heat lemon curd in a small saucepan, stirring constantly, until heated through. Drizzle lemon curd over pancakes and top with a few fresh raspberries.

Prosciutto Wrapped, Gorgonzola Stuffed Dates With Balsamic Honey Syrup

Ingredients:

For the Dates:

20 Dates, pitted

4 ounces Gorgonzola cheese

1 6-ounce package Prosciutto, sliced lengthwise

For the Syrup:

1 cup Balsamic Vinegar

3 Tablespoons Honey

Directions for the dates:

1. Preheat oven to 350°F.
2. Slice one side of the dates and stuff with cheese.

3. Wrap each date with a piece of prosciutto and place on foil-lines sheet pan. Bake for 15 minutes.

For the syrup:

1. Place the vinegar and honey in a small saucepan.
2. Simmer over medium heat, stirring constantly, until liquid is reduced by half and has thickened, about 20 minutes.
3. Drizzle syrup over dates. The dates can be served warm or at room temperature.

Roasted Eggplant Spread

Ingredients:

 2 medium eggplants, sliced into 1 inch rounds
 3/4 cup extra virgin olive oil, divided
 1 large yellow onion, sliced thin (about 2 cups)
 1 clove garlic, minced
 Salt and pepper to taste

Directions:

1. Heat oven to 450°F. Drizzle 1/4 cup olive oil over eggplant rounds and roast in hot oven until golden brown and soft, about 30 minutes, turning midway through the roasting process.

2. While eggplant is roasting, heat a frying pan over medium flame. Add 1/4 cup olive oil and

the onions to the pan. Turn down heat to medium low and cook for 10 minutes. Add the garlic to the pan. Cook another 10 minutes or until onion is golden brown.

3. Scrape the eggplant meat from the skin. Place the roasted eggplant in a food processor along with the onions and the final ¼ cup oil. Season with salt and pepper. Process to a spreading consistency. Serve with crusty bread.

Black Olive and Artichoke Spread

Ingredients:
    2 15-ounce can chick peas, rinsed and drained
    1 cup black olives, pitted and chopped
    1 12-ounce jar of marinated artichoke hearts, drained
    1/4 cup extra virgin olive oil
    Salt and pepper (optional)

Directions:
Place all ingredients in a food processor and process to a spreading consistency. Check for seasoning. If salt and pepper are needed, add a bit and process a bit longer. Serve with crusty bread.

Smith Island Cake

Ingredients:

For the cake:

1 cup butter, room temperature

3 cups all-purpose flour

1 teaspoon salt

2 teaspoons baking powder

2 cups sugar

5 large eggs

1 1/2 cups milk

2 teaspoons vanilla extract

For the icing:

2 cups sugar

1 cup evaporated milk

5 ounces unsweetened chocolate, chopped

1/2 cup butter

2 teaspoon vanilla

Directions:

1. Pre-heat oven to 350°F. Prepare 10 9-inch round cake pans with non-stick cooking spray. If you don't have 10 pans, you can cook the layers in batches using 2 or 3 pans.
2. Prepare the cake batter: Whisk together the flour, salt, and baking powder. In a second bowl, combine the butter and sugar, beating until light and fluffy. Add eggs one at a time and beat until well incorporated.
3. Add the flour and the milk to the butter mixture, and stir until just combined.
4. Put 2/3 cup of the batter into each pan. Use the back of the spoon to spread it evenly, then tap the pans on the counter until batter is evenly distributed. This step is crucial to having nice, even cake layers. Bake in the middle of the oven for 8-11 minutes. Cake will pull away from the sides of the pan a bit when fully cooked. Remove from oven. Let sit for a few minutes. Remove cakes from pans and set aside to cool.
5. For the icing: Combine the sugar and milk in

a medium saucepan. Add the chocolate and butter. Over medium-low heat, warm through, stirring constantly, until sugar is dissolved, and chocolate and butter are melted. Increase the heat to medium and cook for about 15 minutes, stirring occasionally. Remove from heat and stir in the vanilla. The icing will thicken as it cools.

6. Place the first cake layer on a plate and ice with 2 or 3 tablespoons of icing, spreading to the edges. Keep adding cake layers and icing. Ice the top and sides with remaining icing.

Other Books by Donna Fasano

Ocean City Boardwalk Series:
Following His Heart, Book 1
Two Hearts in Winter, Book 2
Wild Hearts of Summer, Book 3
An Almost Perfect Christmas, Book 4
Grown-Up Christmas List, Book 5
The Wedding Planner's Son, Book 6

~ ~ ~

Reclaim My Heart
The Merry-Go-Round
Her Fake Romance
Take Me, I'm Yours
His Wife for a While
An Accidental Family
Mountain Laurel

~ ~ ~

OTHER BOOKS BY DONNA FASANO

The Single Daddy Club Series:
Derrick, Book 1
Jason, Book 2
Reece, Book 3

~ ~ ~

A Family Forever Series:
A Beautiful Stranger, Book 1
Made in Paradise, Book 2
Other titles coming soon

Non-fiction Books
Cooking In All Directions
Prayer of Quiet
Favorite Christmas Cookies
Recipes of Love
Guy Food

About The Author

Donna Fasano is a USA TODAY Bestselling Author whose books have sold nearly 4 million copies worldwide and have been translated into two dozen languages. She lives on Maryland's Eastern Shore with her husband Bill and Roo, their thirteen-year-old Australian cattle dog mix.